"Don't presume to [know me]
so well," Nikki sai[d]

"Oh, I know you." Alex stopped pacing. Stared at her in the firelight. "And I know that out of all the women in my life you're the only one I ever counted on. And you walked out without one single reason that I can accept. Was I really that impossible to work with, Nik?"

"You didn't do anything." Nikki's voice was husky.

"But someone did. Was it the father of your baby?"

"Just…leave it alone, please."

"You're just letting this yahoo walk. Without taking any responsibility at all for the baby."

"It doesn't concern you!"

He inhaled. Exhaled more slowly. "Then why does it feel as if it does?"

Nikki didn't answer.

And Alex knew he was right. If he weren't, she would have said so. But knowing it with more certainty than ever didn't make him feel any better.

Dear Reader,

Well, it's September, which always sounds like a fresh start to me, no matter how old I get. And evidently we have six women this month who agree. In *Home Again* by Joan Elliott Pickart, a woman who can't have children has decided to work with them in a professional capacity—but when she is assigned an orphaned little boy, she fears she's in over her head. Then she meets his gorgeous guardian—and she's *sure* of it!

In the next installment of MOST LIKELY TO…, *The Measure of a Man* by Marie Ferrarella, a single mother attempting to help her beloved former professor joins forces with a former campus golden boy, now the college…custodian. What could have happened? Allison Leigh's *The Tycoon's Marriage Bid* pits a pregnant secretary against her ex-boss who, unbeknownst to him, has a real connection to her baby's father. In *The Other Side of Paradise* by Laurie Paige, next up in her SEVEN DEVILS miniseries, a mysterious woman seeking refuge as a ranch hand learns that she may have more ties to the community than she could have ever suspected. When a beautiful nurse is assigned to care for a devastatingly handsome, if cantankerous, cowboy, the results are…well, you get the picture—but you can have it spelled out for you in Stella Bagwell's next MEN OF THE WEST book, *Taming a Dark Horse*. And in *Undercover Nanny* by Wendy Warren, a domestically challenged female detective decides it's necessary to penetrate the lair of single father and heir to a grocery fortune by pretending to be…his nanny. Hmm. It *could* work.…

So enjoy, and snuggle up. Fall weather is just around the corner.…

Happy reading!

Gail Chasan
Senior Editor

Please address questions and book requests to:
Silhouette Reader Service
U.S.: 3010 Walden Ave., P.O. Box 1325, Buffalo, NY 14269
Canadian: P.O. Box 609, Fort Erie, Ont. L2A 5X3

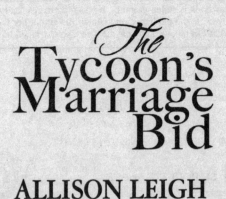

ALLISON LEIGH

Silhouette®

SPECIAL EDITION®

Published by Silhouette Books

America's Publisher of Contemporary Romance

For my family.
Always.

SILHOUETTE BOOKS

ISBN 0-373-24707-9

THE TYCOON'S MARRIAGE BID

Visit Silhouette Books at www.eHarlequin.com

Printed in U.S.A.

ALLISON LEIGH

started early by writing a Halloween play that her grade-school class performed. Since then, though her tastes have changed, her love for reading has not. And her writing appetite simply grows more voracious by the day.

She has been a finalist in the RITA® Award and the Holt Medallion contests. But the true highlights of her day as a writer are when she receives word from a reader that they laughed, cried or lost a night of sleep while reading one of her books.

Born in Southern California, Allison has lived in several different cities in four different states. She has been, at one time or another, a cosmetologist, a computer programmer and a secretary. She has recently begun writing full-time after spending nearly a decade as an administrative assistant for a busy neighborhood church, and currently makes her home in Arizona with her family. She loves to hear from her readers, who can write to her at P.O. Box 40772, Mesa, AZ 85274-0772.

GRANDMA'S 20-MINUTE BROWNIE RECIPE

2 squares unsweetened baking chocolate
½ cup butter
3 eggs
1 cup sugar
¾ cup flour
½ tsp baking powder
¼ tsp salt
½ tsp vanilla
1 cup chopped nuts

Preheat oven to 350° F.

Melt chocolate and butter. Cool. Beat eggs 5 minutes. Add sugar and beat again. Sift dry ingredients and add to egg mixture. Add melted chocolate mixture. Add vanilla and nuts. Spread in a greased 9"x13" pan and bake at 350° F for 20 minutes. Can dust top lightly with powered sugar. Cut and remove from pan while hot.

Chapter One

Nikki Day didn't want to open her eyes. Not when doing so would confirm that *yes,* she was very much in a hospital bed, and now she was losing her mind, to boot. Because there was no way on earth that *he* would really be sitting there in the recliner next to the bed as if he belonged there.

Which meant she was seeing things.

Hallucinating.

As if she didn't have enough worries already.

Her arm curled protectively over her abdomen as she felt another hard kick. At least that movement assured her that whatever was happening and *why* ever she was here, the baby was now gunning for kicker of the year. Nikki was in her sixth month. She figured by the time she made it to nine, the baby would be leaving behind permanent footprints—her own personal Hollywood Walk of Fame.

She gingerly shifted to her side, pushing a pillow against her abdomen, trying to find a more comfortable position, and regrettably opened her eyes as she did so.

He was still there.

Dismay shot through her and she hurriedly closed them again.

Tightly.

"Nice to see you, too," the apparition said in a low voice.

It appeared that when Nikki hallucinated, she could do it with as much accuracy and precision as she'd done most things in her life.

The realization made her want to laugh. Was she hysterical?

She shifted again, wishing she could escape the ache in her back as much as she wished she could escape the rabbit hole she'd fallen down.

"Careful. You don't want to yank out that IV line."

She nearly came out of her skin when those long, capable…*warm* fingers settled over her hand.

Definitely not a hallucination.

She jerked back, sitting up so abruptly the pale blue sheet fell to her waist, displaying a limp, blue cotton hospital gown. The pillow teetered on the edge of the bed, then slid over.

He still held her hand, though. He was evidently concerned about the thin tubing snaking from beneath the adhesive on the back of her hand, because there was no other reason he'd have held her so.

He. Alexander Reed. Alex.

The man who was—inadvertently and completely unknowingly—responsible for the baby that was even now kicking the life out of her kidneys.

He'd been her boss for three years, until she'd resigned last summer.

Nikki's heart pounded so hard she felt faint.

"Easy there," he murmured, casually reaching for the button that hung from a cord near her shoulder. "Don't upset yourself. You're fine. The baby's fine."

She swallowed, his assurance calming the panic roiling inside her. The baby. Concentrate on the baby.

She carefully pulled her hand from beneath his. "How did I get back to Cheyenne?"

He shook his head. "You didn't. You're still in Montana. Lucius Community Hospital."

"You sure are," the nurse entering the room agreed. "And we're happy to see you're awake." She smiled comfortingly as she bustled around the bed, checking machines and making notes. "The doctor will be right in," she told Alex as she deftly wrapped Nikki's arm in a blood pressure cuff. "We're a little busy today. Two babies on the way." She finished with the cuff and made some more notes. "How are you feeling, hon?"

Nikki couldn't formulate a coherent answer. But the nurse seemed to understand. "Just remain quiet," she told her. "The doctor won't be long."

When the nurse departed, Nikki eyed Alex again. "What are *you* doing here?" Never mind what *she* was doing there. Not even the nurse had helped to answer that question.

Alex's dark brown eyes were as unreadable as ever. "They called me when you were brought in."

"They?"

He moved his shoulders slightly as if he were impatient with the question. She wasn't surprised. When she'd worked for him, Alex had depended on *her* to handle the details. The man wouldn't remember his own birthday if she hadn't reminded him to check his calendar.

"The woman who owns that inn you were staying at," he said. "The only phone number she had, other than your home, was your work number. The hospital called me, too."

Her *former* work number. "Hadley Golightly?" Nikki wasn't only trying to get details out of him. She was trying not to betray the fact that she was desperately trying to recall what had happened. "Tiff's is a boardinghouse. Not an inn."

"Fine. A boardinghouse." Alex's sharp gaze had strayed to the window. Narrow blinds covered it, slanted so the sun wouldn't shine directly into the room. Not that there was any sun, from the looks of it. Just gray skies, heavy with snow. Typical January whether she was home in Wyoming or vacationing in Montana.

Her temples throbbed. "The baby," she whispered. "You're sure about the baby?"

"I'm sure." He looked back at her, and the steadiness of his gaze eased her as much as his words did.

"I still don't understand what *you're* doing here, though." Why hadn't Alex called her family rather than come to Montana himself? It wasn't as if he didn't know who they were. Her sister, Belle, had worked for him at Huffington Sports Clinic, too. For a while, at least.

The whispery details of a blue, horse-drawn sleigh straight out of a fairy tale drifted in and out of her mind, as insubstantial as a curl of smoke.

Cody had promised her a sleigh ride for their honeymoon.

But that was years ago.

Nikki had gone on the sleigh ride alone. It was the last thing she remembered. Sitting on the thickly padded seat, the morning air bright and crisp on her face.

Or was that a dream, too?

She couldn't seem to concentrate on more than one thing at a time, and the elusive details slipped away.

Would it be easier to deal with Alex than her foggy memory?

Probably not.

What was he really doing here?

She'd already removed herself from his life once.

This was backtracking in the worst of ways.

"How…how are things at the office?" She couldn't seem to prevent the question from emerging any more than she could prevent the nerves jangling through the muzziness fogging her brain.

"Had to let another admin go last week."

"Another one?" She'd heard the rumblings, of course, about Alex's difficulty in hiring a permanent replacement for her. No matter how well she'd thought she'd excised Huffington from her life—and the man who'd taken one small Wyoming clinic and turned it into an innovative network spread across the United States— she'd still heard that, after she'd left, he'd gone through his first three administrative assistants in as many weeks. "What number was she?"

His lips pursed a little. It only made her notice them, which she had no business doing. "Six." His gaze slanted from the window back to her bed.

She braced herself. Even though he'd never really seemed to notice her, it had always given Nikki a jolt whenever he'd looked at her.

She'd almost not taken the administrative assistant position in the first place, as a result of that. She hadn't *wanted* to feel any sort of jolt from anyone. Not when Cody was still in her heart.

The jolt was there. As usual.

A dip, a sway, a leap. Deep inside her.

More than three and a half years since the April day she'd sat across from Alex's desk and accepted the position, and it was as bad—or worse—than ever.

"How's, um, how's everything else with the clinics, then?" Her voice was a little breathless. She hoped he'd think it had something to do with whatever had put her in the hospital.

Knowing Alex, he knew more about those details than she.

His expression didn't change. "You think I came here to discuss business?"

"You called me nearly five times a week at first to discuss business." He'd stopped calling after that first month, though.

She'd breathed easier, but grieved a little harder for the job she'd really loved.

"I wouldn't have had to make those calls if the personnel department had a clue about hiring someone competent."

"It's your personnel department," she replied mildly. Huffington was entirely Alex's baby. There was no higher authority in the company.

She had a fanciful image of herself hovering around the ceiling of the hospital room, watching this particular exchange. Discussing *business?*

The baby kicked again and she dragged her split persona down from the ceiling. "So…you came here to… what? Ask me to come back to my job?"

"You still consider being my administrative assistant your job?"

She shifted her shoulders. "No."

"Then you're employed elsewhere now."

"I start a job very soon." She hoped, desperately wishing she knew how *long* she'd been in the hospital. She'd been living on her savings for months, and her pride simply refused to let her take handouts from her family, no matter how easily they could have afforded it.

She was Nikki Day. She stood on her own two feet. The practice had kept her together when she and

Belle were only fifteen and their father died, and it had kept her together again when Cody died just as unexpectedly.

She needed the job she was supposed to begin after this trip to Montana.

"A job."

She had to gather her scattered thoughts again. It was about as easy as gathering up sand with a sieve. "Yes."

"Where?"

His disbelief wasn't at all flattering. "It's none of your business, Alex." She'd have prided herself on the statement if her voice hadn't trembled.

He looked disbelieving, but let it slide. Probably out of whatever pity had motivated him to come to the hospital. Then he glanced at his watch. Not overly noticeably, except that she knew him so well, having worked fifty- to sixty-hour weeks for him for three years.

She'd taken one week of vacation during her second year with Huffington. She and Belle had gone to Florida. If she hadn't made the mistake of taking her cell phone with her, she might actually have managed to leave work behind. Instead, her sister had come back far tanner than Nikki, with a little album full of pictures of herself scuba diving and parasailing.

Nikki had come back knowing the room service menu by heart.

She hadn't bothered trying to take a vacation again.

"Don't let me keep you," she said now. She was desperately eager for him to leave, and painfully aware that she was doing a miserable job of hiding it.

He lifted one slashing eyebrow. "What'd I do to piss you off, Nikki?"

"Nothing!"

"Right."

His dark gaze drifted downward from her face and she felt the heat of a fresh flush. She had to look as washed out as she felt.

She was used to being in control of things. Of herself.

Now, adrift in a tangle of pale blue sheets, she felt completely at a loss.

"Did you quit because of your pregnancy?"

"Of course not," she exclaimed rapidly. Truthfully. The fact was, when she'd quit, she'd typed up her resignation and placed it square in the center of his computer keyboard—where he'd be *certain* to see it—before she'd realized she was pregnant.

Had she known, she still would have handed in her notice.

"You could have told me you were pregnant. I would have made some adjustments," he said, ignoring her denial. He scooped up the pillow from the floor and set it on the bed beside her. "Maybe hired an assistant."

"That's what you did," she pointed out. She pushed the pillow behind her. "I quit. You hired another admin. Simple."

"Hired *you* an assistant." His lips compressed a little, and the slashing dimple in his hard cheek flashed. "So you could work fewer hours or something."

Alex had never once concerned himself with how many hours she'd put in for him. She was back to hal-

lucinating again. Or maybe she'd wake up and find herself sitting with her nose in her computer outside Alex's
office, and that the last half year had been nothing more
than a long, incredibly vivid nightmare.

She rubbed her temples.

"You didn't have to quit on me," Alex said.

Quitting was exactly what she'd had to do. And there
was no way on earth she'd ever be able to explain that
fact to him.

She dropped her hands to her lap and leaned weari-
ly against the pillow behind her. She pulled the limp
sheet and thin blanket up to her shoulders.

She wasn't cold. She just needed more of a barrier
between them.

She'd been a good administrative assistant. But nobody was irreplaceable. "I still don't understand what
you're doing here."

"Your sister is on her honeymoon."

She frowned, wondering how he'd known that. "Yes."

"Your mom and her husband are on some cruise or
something."

Her mother had spent months planning the vacation.
Squire, Nikki was convinced, had only agreed to plant
his cowboy boots on a cruise ship deck because of the
wife he adored. "Yes," she confirmed warily. "But
what's that have to do with you?"

His shoulders moved again. He stood and walked to
the foot of the bed. "So I came to Montana," he said flatly. "Someone needed to."

He'd hardly explained his actions. Aside from her

twin sister and her mother, he knew she had a sizable stepfamily. Any one of the Clays would have assisted her in any way they could, just as she knew, without question, that she'd have abhorred even asking.

But Alex didn't know that. And he never did anything without an agenda.

Not that he couldn't be kind when he chose. She knew only too well how many philanthropic efforts he'd been involved in, the boards on which he sat. Chaired. Organized. All located in the nine cities— from Florida to Arizona—where Huffington clinics were situated.

But mostly, Alex ate, breathed and slept his business. If she hadn't been his administrative assistant, he'd have never noticed her.

"Well." She settled her palms flat on the blanket beside her hips. "I appreciate your concern, but as you can see, I'm fine."

"A polite way of telling me I can just toddle on out the door now?" His voice was dry.

She winced. Flushed, yet again. "Alex, this is just…embarrassing for me," she admitted.

"Why?"

Her hands were no longer flat. They curled, bunched into fists, as Nikki wished the ground would swallow her whole. "How would you feel if I walked in on you in the hospital?"

He tucked his hands in his pockets, but the action did little to mar the line of his perfectly tailored black trousers. "Perhaps glad to see a familiar face."

She felt her cheeks flame even hotter. "Now you're making me sound ungrateful."

"If the shoe fits."

There was a knot constricting her throat. "Please don't try guilting me into coming back, Alex." She wasn't sure she could withstand it again.

"It didn't work when I tried before." He stepped across the room and pulled one hand out of his pocket to adjust the window blinds.

More gray light entered the room, and Nikki realized she was staring at the subtle play of muscles beneath Alex's ivory sweater. Cashmere, undoubtedly, considering the way the soft garment draped his broad shoulders.

His hair was black, tipped by silver around his temples. His nape, too, if he went a week too long between haircuts. But now it was cut as short as ever. Then those salt-and-pepper strands turned, and she swallowed, caught gawking, when he looked back at her.

Not that he made any mention of her staring.

"I came because I was concerned," he said mildly. "So. Is there someone you'd prefer to have called?" One eyebrow lifted, his chocolate eyes shifting to her midsection. "Maybe the guy who did that?"

She looked down at her hands. They were puffy. She'd stopped wearing all her rings a month ago. Even the amethyst promise ring that Cody had given her.

"He's gone," she said. And she refused to get any more detailed. "I do appreciate the fact that you came up here from Cheyenne, Alex. I know how busy you are. But I'm *fine*."

He just watched her.

Well, okay, she was lying in a hospital bed, so obviously things weren't all tulips and daisies. "I'll *be* fine," she amended.

"You don't even know what happened."

As long as she felt the baby kicking away inside her, she figured she could deal with whatever had happened. What she couldn't deal with was facing Alex for any length of time. "Do *you* know?"

He wasn't a family member. He wasn't even her employer anymore. The hospital shouldn't have divulged any of her personal information to him.

But she knew Alex had a way of getting what he wanted.

"I know enough," he said.

A statement that did not alleviate any of the nerves jostling inside her. "Meaning what?"

"You were far more agreeable when you worked for me."

"You paid me to be agreeable." Again, her voice was shaking.

"Right. Well, nobody knows more than I do just how capable you are, Nikki." He scooped up a black coat she recognized from the seat of a rolling metal stool stuck in the corner. "You'll undoubtedly improve efficiency around here by thirty percent before you're released. The staff will be completely whipped into shape." Now his tone wasn't kind at all.

It was tight.

Angry.

And it stunned the life out of her.

What did he have to be angry about?

"Alex. Wait." The words burst from her lips even as caution screamed inside her.

She wanted him to leave.

Didn't she?

"Please," she whispered. "Wait."

No matter how desperate she was to regain some composure, she couldn't abide the idea of having angered him. Regardless of his motives, he'd come here.

She'd never known him to take any time away from his business.

Not for anyone. So why had he done it for her?

Chapter Two

Before Alex could respond, a doctor came into the room and took in both of them with a glance. "Good. You're finally awake. Since you're both here, we need to go over Mom's options after I examine her."

Which told Nikki *ever* so much.

And she had no idea if Alex would have stayed because of her request, or not.

The gangly doctor—he briskly introduced himself as Dr. Carmichael—set the thick chart he was holding on the rolling table at the base of Nikki's bed, and stepped up beside her, whipping out his stethoscope with one hand and nudging up his round eyeglasses with the other.

Before Nikki could utter a word, he'd plucked the string holding her hospital gown together at her neck, and nudged her forward a little. The stethoscope was cold against her back and she hurriedly grabbed the front of the gown before it fell completely off her shoulders.

She *couldn't* look at Alex now.

Just as quickly, Dr. Carmichael nudged her back against the pillows again, murmuring periodic "mmm-hmms" as he delved beneath the neck of the gown to listen to her heartbeat.

Her face was on fire.

She knew her pulse was racing, and it had nothing whatsoever to do with the doctor, who'd already withdrawn his cold stethoscope and transferred his attention to feeling along her jaw and neck, for heaven only knew what.

His mmm-hmming kept on until he stepped back to the foot of the bed, flipped open the chart and made a few notations. The same nurse came into the room then and gently shooed Alex out long enough for the doctor to do a pelvic exam.

When he was finished, the doctor scooted back on his rolling stool, disposing of his sterile gloves. "Looking good. Spotting has stopped."

The nurse finished deftly adjusting the bedding and retied the back of the deplorable gown, since Nikki was too busy staring at the doctor to deal with it herself. "I was spotting? How long have I been here?" She would remember if she'd been spotting!

"Four days now," the nurse said calmly. "You were brought in on Sunday. It's Thursday. Your Mr. Reed has stayed by your side since he arrived Tuesday. Half the nurses in the hospital are pea green with envy, I can tell you."

Four days?

She'd been thinking maybe four hours.

Distress gnawed at her.

The doctor was still sitting, and the overhead light glinted off his glasses as he waved Alex in when the nurse opened the door once more. "As I was telling Nikki, the spotting has stopped. There's been no evidence of any more contractions."

"More?" Her voice rose at that.

Just what had been going on while she was unconscious?

The nurse patted her arm. "Try not to get excited, hon. Your blood pressure was through the roof when the ambulance brought you in. It's only begun to stabilize in the last twelve hours."

News that was *not* helping Nikki become any calmer. "The baby's been moving," she said nervously. Alex had told her she and the baby were fine. "So what's wrong?"

"Nothing that bed rest won't cure, I believe," the doctor assured her. He adjusted his glasses, making them glint again. "Frankly, at this point, the baby is healthier than you are."

"Then I can go home?"

"I'd prefer to keep you here in the hospital. I want you off your feet for the next three weeks." He glanced at her chart again. "You'll be in your third trimester then."

Nikki's stomach dived down to her toes. Her new job came equipped with medical insurance coverage—which she would desperately need by the time her delivery date arrived—but not until she'd actually been working there for sixty days. *Working* being the operative word.

If she was here in this Montana hospital for weeks, she couldn't very well report for her first day at Belvedere Salvage & Wrecking on Monday, now could she?

"But that won't do," she said faintly.

"I'm afraid it's going to have to do," Dr. Carmichael said, unperturbed. He patted her foot through the blanket. "Don't worry. The food here will grow on you."

The knot in her throat had become a vise, and it seemed to be forcing every bit of liquid inside her up behind her eyes.

The doctor wasn't entirely oblivious to her upset. "It won't be so bad. After the first week, we'll reevaluate. And Dad can stay with you as long as he wants, same as he's been doing."

Nikki eyed Alex. His long form wavered. The doctor figured he was telling her things that would make her feel better.

But Alex *wasn't* the expectant father. How could he be when there had never been anything remotely personal between them?

But he wasn't disputing the doctor's assumption, either.

"I can't afford to stay three weeks in the hospital." She pushed out the words, trying to pretend that *he* wasn't standing there listening. "I have to get home. I have to work."

The doctor looked at her over the rims of his glasses. "I can't force you to stay, of course. But I promise you that you'll be endangering your pregnancy if you do not have complete bed rest."

Endangering.

The word rocketed around inside her like some bizarre pinball machine running amok, setting off small explosions wherever the ball hit.

"She could get the bed rest elsewhere, though." Alex finally spoke up. "Correct?"

The doctor didn't look particularly happy about it, but he nodded. "If she can promise me that she'll remain in bed. And I mean *lying* in bed. Knees elevated. She can sit up for a few minutes at a time, but that's it."

"I'll go to my mother's," Nikki said thickly. Her family would welcome her with open arms, without question. And she'd feel like she was failing them by not being able to stand on her own two feet the way she always had.

"Your mother lives here in Lucius?"

"No. Wyoming."

Before she'd finished speaking, the doctor was shaking his head. "No travel. Not even an hour."

"But—"

"Don't argue, Nikki." Alex's voice was smooth. "We'll do whatever is necessary to protect the baby."

"We?" Her hands clutched the blanket, bunching it frantically. The monitor beside her began bleating like an angry lamb, and spewed out a stream of narrow paper.

"Ms. Day." The nurse gently nudged her back against the pillows. "Please. Don't excite yourself."

Nikki waved her hand at the doctor. "You just sentence me to bed rest for the better part of a month and I'm not supposed to get excited?" A sharp pain tore through her midsection and she exhaled loudly, drawing up her knees, doubling over.

The nurse and Dr. Carmichael were suddenly all business. Blood pressure cuffs. Syringes.

Nikki didn't much notice what they did, since panic was rocketing through her, keeping company with the grappling hook that was twisting her insides into a knot.

The baby had been a complete accident.

But that didn't mean she didn't want it.

Oh God oh God oh God.

Alex slid his hand into hers.

She stared blindly at him. The pain was excruciating.

"Nikki…" His voice was soft. Insistent.

She blinked. Focused. The panic retreated a hair. She was hardly aware of the death grip her fingers had on his. "It hurts," she gasped.

His intense gaze was steady. Calm.

Familiar.

"I know. Relax." His voice was almost hypnotic. "Everything is going to be fine."

She was twenty-seven years old. A modern, competent, independent woman. She didn't need anyone to tell her that everything would be fine.

She was the one who usually made certain that things *were* fine.

Only none of that amounted to a hill of beans right now.

She was glad he was there. Glad. Pathetically glad.

Her tears slipped out, streaming down her cheeks. She'd never once cried in front of her boss.

No. He wasn't her boss any longer.

He was just Alex.

A man she still couldn't manage to get out of her head.

"Breathe," he told her. She was vaguely aware that the nurse had been repeating the same thing.

She drew in a slow breath.

"That's it," he said encouragingly. "Slow and easy."

The grappling hook was slowly, infinitesimally, loosening.

"I don't want to lose the baby." Her voice was thick.

His brown gaze didn't flicker. His hand never let go of hers. "I won't let that happen," he promised.

It made no sense. But she believed him.

"Try and lie back, Ms. Day."

She felt woozy. Incapable of making herself uncurl. Focusing on Alex's face was getting harder. But when he leaned over her, gently settling her back against the pillows, she could still make out the subtle variations of brown in his eyes.

Dark, clear coffee rimmed by a narrow circle of chocolate Kisses.

"Melted," she corrected. Melted chocolate. Rich. Thick. Addictive.

He was still so close. "Melted what?"

She frowned a little. Had she said it out loud? "My head feels funny."

"It's the sedative," the nurse stated. She unwrapped the blood pressure cuff from Nikki's arm and tucked the contraption back in its holder beside the bed. "Don't worry. It won't harm the baby. You're just both going to have a little nap."

"I don't want a nap. I have to go back to Cheyenne."

"Not today you don't. You've been out of it for four days, remember?" Alex let go of her and straightened, moving away from the bed.

She wanted to call him back. But the idea took too much effort.

Later. She'd call him later.

No, she wouldn't call him back later.

Later she'd have to call human resources at Belvedere and see if she could salvage the job she was supposed to start.

Salvage.

She felt an amused giggle rise in her, but it never seemed to make it out.

She'd have to do lots of things.

She just couldn't put her finger on what they were at the moment....

Alex watched Nikki's eyes close. The stress wrinkling her forehead smoothed out. Her lips softened.

"She'll sleep for a few hours," the nurse told him quietly.

Alex nodded. He followed the doctor outside the room. "You've been running tests on her since I got here. I want details." He wasn't a physician himself, but he came from a long line of them, and he employed a fair number himself. If he wasn't satisfied with the doctor's answers, he'd have Nikki under someone else's care in a heartbeat.

"We can talk in my office," the doctor said easily. "I wouldn't mind getting some medical history on you, as well."

Alex smiled noncommittally. It suited him to let the doctor believe he was the baby's father. If the other man knew just how nonpersonal his relationship with Nikki Day was, Alex would have a harder time getting the information he wanted.

He'd still get it.

He just preferred to get it as expediently as possible.

He should have done it all when he'd arrived at the hospital. Instead, he'd sat by Nikki's bedside.

It was unfathomable even to him.

Two hours later, he'd obtained all the details of Nikki's and her baby's health that he wanted. He'd even called his uncle, who was head of obstetrics for RHS Memorial, the Philadelphia flagship hospital of Reed Health Systems, who concurred with Dr. Carmichael's plan of treatment.

Alex had plenty of disagreements with his family. But when it came to basic medical care, there were few minds finer.

So he sat now in the recliner in Nikki's room, watching her sleep. There was a little more color in her face than there had been when he'd first arrived.

His first sight of her had hit him in a way he was still trying to figure out. When she'd worked for him, he'd never seen her with a hair on her auburn head out of place, and he'd never seen her lose her composure. Not with temper or tears. She'd been efficient as hell. The best assistant he could ever have wanted. She'd kept his hectic life in order, and he was still reeling all these months after she'd left him flat.

It wasn't a fact he particularly liked admitting, either. He didn't like depending on anyone. Not when they invariably failed you.

But he'd depended on Nikki.

Right now, she seemed miles away from that fearsomely competent young woman who'd often beat him to the office in the mornings, and generally outlasted him at the end of the day. Aside from the swollen soccer-ball-size mound her slender arm was curled protectively over, she seemed too thin, and ridiculously young.

Vulnerable.

Her hair waved across the white pillow in a fiery river, looking more red than brown. There were no cosmetics to make her ivory complexion perfect, and it was smooth as velvet anyway. Her lips were softly parted and her oval chin was relaxed, missing its typical nononsense tilt.

Nikki Day was beautiful.

He supposed that wasn't really a news flash to him. The vulnerability, though. That was as unexpected as finding her pregnant.

Which didn't explain, even to him, what he was doing here.

Nikki was right to be surprised. Suspicious, even.

He had a dozen things—give or take a hundred—to deal with regarding Huffington. He hadn't been exaggerating about the competence of the assistants that HR had been sending his way. And having a barely tolerable assistant just now was worse than having no assistant.

Nikki shifted, turning on her side, and tucked her hand against her cheek. Beneath the thin blanket, her leg moved, and the bare tips of her toes sneaked out from beneath the covers. Her toenails were painted a soft peach color.

His favorite fruit had always been peaches.

Annoyed with the thought, he looked back at her face.

Her eyes were open. Dark blue. Slightly unfocused. But they cleared almost instantly.

"It's not some bad dream?" Her voice was little more than a soft sigh.

He shook his head and hoped to hell those blue eyes didn't fill with tears again. Seeing Nikki Day in tears unnerved him. It wasn't a sensation he welcomed. "No. How're you feeling?"

"Woozy." One slender arm was still crossed protectively over her abdomen.

"The baby's okay. And Carmichael has been in contact with your OB in Cheyenne."

She looked distinctly discomfited at the news. "I probably don't want to know how you know that, nor how Dr. Carmichael even knows *who* my doctor there is, do I?"

Since that was true, he kept silent.

She turned on her back. Started to fold her arm over

her eyes but didn't, giving the IV taped to it a baleful look. "Belle and Cage got married before Christmas. They put off their honeymoon until after the holidays. If I call them now, they won't have a chance to get away again until summer, and then…"

Calling her sister was the logical answer. Yet she sounded miserable over it.

"Where'd they go for their honeymoon?" he asked.

"The Caribbean."

Her eyes *were* wet. Damn.

"Belle was so excited. Not just because it's her honeymoon, but because she's always dreamed of traveling to places like that. But at least they're probably reachable." Nikki's voice went a little hoarse. "My mother and Squire are floating somewhere on the Mediterranean. I know they can be reached in an emergency, but—"

He lifted his hand. He *really* didn't like seeing tears in her eyes. "You don't have to reach anyone."

She shook her head. The tears glinted. "I can't afford one week in the hospital, much less three."

He could tell reiterating the admission cost her. Not that he hadn't figured it out for himself. She hadn't been working anywhere in Cheyenne—not that he'd been able to discover, anyway. And to his chagrin, he'd tried. He knew her mother's husband had money, but he also figured that asking for help was not Nikki's particular forte.

Since he was generally more in the position of cleaning up other people's messes than being in need of cleaning in his own life, he figured that was something they had in common.

When had Nikki had time for any sort of personal life?
The thought kept coming to the forefront.

He'd kept her too busy for a personal life.

Or so he'd thought.

He marshaled his thoughts. "I've rented you a place."

Silence descended on the room as she absorbed his statement. Then her eyes widened. Color touched, then just as quickly fled from her cheeks. "Excuse me?"

"I took care of it while you were sleeping. The sheriff's office recommended a few places. Someone from the inn packed up your stuff, and it's been moved to the rental." He figured just about any place would be better than the Lucius Inn, which didn't even possess a proper suite.

"How…efficient."

"Then it's settled."

Her eyebrows rose. She pushed herself up on her elbow, and there was nothing dazed in her eyes now. Incredulousness shone clear and sharp.

"No, it's not! How am I supposed to afford—" she waved her hand, a brief motion conveying a wealth of frustration "—this *place* you've arranged? And I'm still going to need help, if I'm supposed to have bed rest. No matter what, I'm going to have to call my family."

"Hold it." He sat forward, resting his arms on his knees. "First of all, I said *I* rented you a place. Period. As for calling your family, you can if you want. I'm just telling you it's not necessary, if you really want to go this alone."

Her brows drew together at that. "Are you going to

hire me a nursemaid, too?" She looked everywhere but at him. "I wasn't *that* perfect of an assistant, Alex. You cannot possibly be so desperate for me to come back to work for you that you'd go to these lengths. I don't want to owe anyone!"

"Anyone, or just me?"

Confusion and pride tangled in her eyes. "Does it matter?"

Did it?

He didn't like owing favors, either. "I'm not hiring a nurse," he said evenly, scrapping the plan to do just that. "I'll stay with you myself."

Chapter Three

Nikki saw Alex's lips move. She heard the words he spoke. But they still made no sense. "*You'll* stay with me," she repeated slowly.

He nodded once.

"Here. In Lucius."

Again, the single nod.

"At this *place* you've rented for me."

A third nod.

She pressed her fingertips to the bridge of her nose, closing her eyes, then opening them again. "That sedative they gave me is really messing with my head."

"No, it's not."

No. It wasn't. If it had been, she'd at least have an

explanation. She dropped her hand to her lap, her palm upward. "I don't want your pity."

His jaw hardened. "You're not getting it. You're an intelligent woman, Nik. This is the easiest solution all the way around."

On the surface, maybe. But spending time—personal time—with Alex? There wasn't anything easy about that, at all.

"What about Huffington?" she asked, determined to keep her tears at bay. She cried far too easily these days. It was maddening.

"What about it?"

It seemed unfathomable, but she could tell by his bland tone that he wasn't going to talk business.

Yet business was the only thing they'd ever had between them.

So what sort of *business* was he up to?

"No," she said abruptly, stomping down on the panic that rose in her at the very thought of him staying with her. "Thank you for the offer, but I really can't accept."

"Why not?"

Her hands flopped. "Because it's not…appropriate!"

His eyebrows rose a little. A muscle twitched at the corner of his lip. "Appropriate," he mused. "Sounding a little virginal there, Nik."

Her face went hot, but she managed to keep her chin up. "I don't care what it sounds like. It's true."

"Definitely more agreeable when you worked for me," he observed. He unfolded from the chair. At six foot four, he was the only man she knew who rivaled her stepbrothers in sheer physical presence. "I have a room at the Lucius Inn. Call me when you change your mind."

"I won't."

His head tilted slightly in acknowledgment. Then he picked up his coat again and left the room. The hospital door swung shut behind him, leaving her alone with nothing but the lingering hint of his aftershave and the rhythmic ticking of the stark round clock hanging very high on the wall.

Maybe the hospital administrators were afraid their patients were likely to abscond with the ugly, utilitarian thing if they hung it at eye level.

She slowly smoothed her hands over the thin blanket, removing every bump and wrinkle. The baby moved. Only a few weeks ago, it had felt more like butterflies darting around inside her. Now, the motions were more distinct. More…real.

She folded her hands over her belly.

Eyed the closed door through the tears that wouldn't be held back no matter how hard she tried, or how desperately she focused on everything around her except her situation.

She would *not* call Alex. She could get through this in the same way she'd gotten through every other painful episode in her life.

On her own. One aching hour…day…week at a time.

Twenty-four hours later, Nikki called Alex at the Lucius Inn.

Twenty-six hours later, she left the hospital—and

very nearly the last chunk of savings she had in her bank account—behind, and was sitting beside him in the luxurious, spacious SUV he'd rented.

She stared out the window beside her as they drove through town. Lucius was a small community, like a dozen others. It had a main drag where most of the businesses seemed to be located. An older, clearly residential area at one end of town. Fortunate evidence of continued growth—a bustling discount department store, apartments, the Lucius Inn, a medical plaza—at the other end of town. She got a good look at all of them when Alex continued driving right on past, leaving the town behind.

She closed her fingers around the softly padded armrest. "Where is this place that you've rented?"

He flicked a glance her way. "Another few miles."

She wanted to ask how few, but didn't. Instead, she turned and stared blindly out the window again.

After a disappointing but unsurprising phone conversation with the salvage company that confirmed they would be unable to hold open the position for her, she'd actually started to call the Caribbean resort where Belle and Cage were staying, but hadn't been able to bring herself to dial the number. What was worse? Calling back her twin from her *honeymoon* or accepting Alex's inconceivable offer?

If Belle and Cage returned, the entire family would be bound to find out about it, and she *hated* worrying them. Hated it. It was bad enough that she knew they'd been worrying over her since she'd announced she was pregnant. They'd harped in the most loving of ways to get her to Weaver or the Double-C, where they could take care of her.

But she took care of herself.

She always had.

But to choose Alex now…that was a different kettle of fish entirely.

Instead of calling Belle, Nikki had left a voice mail message for Emily, one of her stepsisters-in-law, that she'd decided to stay in Montana for a few more weeks, and would call when she got back.

Then she'd hurriedly called Alex.

She still wasn't sure she'd made the right choice, either.

The cadence of the tires on the highway deepened and she looked ahead as Alex slowed and turned off on a narrow road. It had recently been plowed, judging by the freshly turned snow neatly mounded at the sides. Not even a thin layer of white powder marred the single lane, which seemed barely wide enough to accommodate the SUV's bulk.

After another ten minutes or so, the pavement ended, but the SUV took the graded gravel in stride. And before long, Alex pulled to a stop in front of a sprawling cabin.

Enormous logs. Stone foundation. A lone window that would let in only twelve square inches of sunlight at a time.

The place looked as if it had been built as a miniature fortress about a million years ago, and for a moment Nikki found herself longing for the confining hospital room.

Alex propped his wrist over the top of the steering wheel as he peered through the windshield at the structure before them. His long, blunt-tipped fingers slowly drummed on the dashboard.

"The sheriff recommended this place?" Nikki finally asked. It was the only glimmer of hope she held.

"He gave me a list of three places. This was the only one available right now. Owner's name is Tucker. Spends winters in Arizona."

"Maybe I should just go back to the boardinghouse." Not that she knew how she'd pay for it.

She realized she was nibbling at her thumbnail, and hurriedly dropped her hand to her lap.

"Can't." Alex was still looking ahead at the dwelling. He seemed as enthusiastic as she was to actually look inside it.

But then Alex lived on the top floor of the Echelon, the finest hotel in Cheyenne. Well, the entire state of Wyoming, for that matter. The Echelon wasn't enormous, but it was "quality."

"Has she already rented out the room I was using?" Nikki'd had the room reserved for a week, Sunday to Saturday. It was only Friday.

He lifted his shoulder. "Called over there this morning and some girl answered. Said Tiff's is more or less closed for a while. The owner—Hadley—had some personal stuff to take care of."

Nikki was chewing her thumbnail again. "I hope she's okay." Hadley was a nice woman, about Nikki's age. Tiff's hadn't been booming with business by any stretch, and Nikki had felt as if Hadley was more a taker in of strays than a dedicated innkeeper. Still, Nikki had had a reason for wanting to stay at Tiff's. And Hadley had been more than accommodating.

"Town's small enough," Alex murmured. "Gossip would have gotten around fast enough if she weren't okay."

True enough. Her mother's family, the Clays, all lived in or near the small town of Weaver, Wyoming, and Nikki knew how effectively gossip could travel there.

Alex's fingers stopped drumming on the dashboard. "Don't move. I'll take a look inside."

Nikki propped her elbow on the armrest and dropped her chin in her hand. "I'm not going anywhere," she murmured to his back as he got out of the vehicle.

How could she?

She'd been lifted from the hospital bed into a wheelchair to exit the hospital, and then lifted from the chair into the SUV that had been idling, warm and cozy, at the curb outside the hospital entrance.

And Alex had done the lifting.

The doctor's instructions had been adamant. The only thing Nikki was allowed to do was sit up for very brief periods of time every few hours. And use the bathroom more or less under her own steam.

She was embarrassingly grateful for that particular mercy.

Her thumbnail found its way between her teeth again.

She watched Alex go up the rickety-looking steps. The security system consisted of a door key hidden inside the ancient metal mailbox affixed to the wall alongside the door.

He glanced back at the SUV for a moment, then went inside.

Nikki wondered what he was thinking.

When she'd been in his employ, she'd believed she'd been able to anticipate his thoughts.

But now she couldn't. The uncharted waters were too vast for her to navigate.

He'd left the door open, but she could see little inside because of the shadows from the steeply pitched porch roof. Assuring herself that the sheriff would not have recommended a place to Alex that had crumbling floorboards and other hazards he could be encountering in there alone, she focused instead on the landscape.

Dozens of winter-bare trees dotted the land around the cabin. And there were evergreens that seemed to reach a mile into the sky.

She suspected that during the rest of the year, the beauty of the landscape compensated for the stark log cabin. Now, though, the place seemed terribly barren.

And her eyes were burning all over again.

She blinked rapidly and sniffed hard. Enough with the waterworks, already. This was just another unexpected challenge to work through. It wasn't as if it were the only hitch in life she'd ever encountered.

As long as she followed the doctor's instructions, the baby would be fine. As long as she concentrated on *that,* she'd get through this. And when the doctor sprang her, Alex would go on his way again, and she would get on with her life.

Nothing all that different than what she'd been doing since last summer, anyway.

The door beside her opened and she jumped.

Alex released her safety belt. "I'll take you in."

She wasn't sure she wanted to leave the warmth of the SUV, where she could entertain fanciful notions of wriggling behind the wheel and driving off. "Is it as ancient inside as it looks outside?"

"Not exactly." He slid his arms beneath her.

The third time to be carried by him.

She buried her face from her chin up to her nose in the ivory scarf wrapped around her neck, and tried not to breathe. Tried to pretend she wasn't fifteen pounds heavier with baby weight, and tried not to justify just how smoothly Alex traipsed across the snow to the cabin.

Yes, he was a large man. But he was a tycoon, not a lumberjack. Carting her—carting anything—around wasn't really his style.

Yet he managed it with as much style as he did most everything else.

She stifled a sigh, only to hold her breath a moment later when he went up the steps, which creaked ominously. He turned sideways to go through the door, then kicked it shut behind them.

The solid slam seemed to echo inside Nikki's head as she stared in disbelief at the interior.

"Oh…my…word."

Alex didn't comment. He merely crossed the gleaming, wood-planked floor that was partially obscured by a massive leopard-print shag rug, and set her on an enormous sectional couch upholstered in racy red leather. "There's a shed of some sort on the other side of the cabin. I'm going to move the truck there after I bring in the groceries. Then I'll get you some lunch. You okay here for that long?"

She nodded weakly and tucked her hands deeper into the pockets of her ivory coat. Anything that would occupy him long enough for her to regain her composure—scrambled from the unlikely interior of the cabin, as much as the unlikely prospect of Alex cooking—was a good thing.

He shut the door behind him when he left, preserving the little bit of warmth that the interior possessed. Her gaze settled on the soaring stone fireplace that dominated the center of the room. She had little doubt the cabin would warm up considerably when a fire was lit in it.

The cabin would warm.

The mammoth, circular bed that she could see through the empty fireplace had velvety pillows mounded against an enormous black, leather headboard. And *it* would warm.

The heart-shaped whirlpool bathtub that took up a chunk of floor space near the couch would warm.

The kitchen and intimate dining nook with its satiny pine table and chairs would warm.

When she and Cody had been planning their wedding, she'd seen advertisements in the bridal magazines of honeymoon cottages that weren't as blatantly sexual as this place. But sweet Cody had only had one place in mind for their honeymoon. Tiff's. Where *his* parents had spent their honeymoon together.

She jumped a little when Alex entered again, his arms loaded with grocery bags, and she dragged her eyes away from the empty bathtub, feeling as if she'd been caught doing something…scandalous.

There was little in the cabin that couldn't be seen from where she sat on the couch—everything seemed oriented around the fireplace—and she watched him dump the bags on the kitchen counter, then stride back outside.

He hadn't done any shopping personally, of course.

He'd merely stopped outside a grocery store after picking her up at the hospital, and as if by magic, a young clerk had dutifully trotted out with the bags, loaded them in the back of the SUV, collected some bills from Alex and disappeared again.

The world according to Alex Reed.

There were a few closed doors in the cabin, and plenty of windows running along the back side of the structure. Unlike the miserly one she'd seen from the outside, there seemed to be a dozen of them. All large and unadorned and overlooking more trees and a narrow, winding stream.

By the time Alex returned after moving the truck, Nikki hoped she'd managed to wipe most of her shock over the cabin interior from her expression.

Not that he'd have noticed, anyway.

He went straight to the kitchen again and began rummaging around. Opening smooth, walnut-planked cupboard doors. Pushing items into the sleek, stainless-steel-fronted refrigerator.

"Alex?"

His head lifted. He looked at her. She could see him through the slice of space between one corner of the fireplace and a bulging green ficus that stood guard over the far end of the sectional couch.

"*Do* you actually know how to cook?"

His teeth flashed in a surprisingly amused grin. "I can punch a microwave button as well as anyone."

She hesitated a moment. "Um…Alex? That's what you said about using the coffeemaker at Huffington." He'd punched buttons on the commercial-style appliance and the repairman had actually been forced to install a new machine when he'd been unable to fix it. After that, Alex had wisely stayed away from the employee break room.

"We're going to have to take our chances," he said dryly. "This microwave is built-in. Don't think I can move it over there next to you so *you* can do button duty."

She heard the microwave door shut, followed by a few beeps. Alex rummaged around a little longer, then approached her, extending an opaque glass toward her. "Here."

She took it. Looked inside the squat rim. "It's milk. I don't drink milk."

"You're pregnant. You're supposed to drink gallons of it, aren't you?"

She'd managed not to so far, courtesy of the prescription she took daily, which her obstetrician vehemently assured her *were* actually prenatal vitamins and not horse pills.

Alex's expression was much the same as it always was: a hint of amusement underlying his otherwise impervious calm. There was no particular reason for her to take the glass. Certainly not because she wanted to please him or something.

That would be ridiculous.

She was pregnant, so he gave her milk.

She needed to stay off her feet, so he made sure she was able to do so.

Why?

She took the glass and began drinking. He pushed the mirror-topped, iron coffee table closer to her end of the couch before returning to the kitchen. Several minutes later, he was back again, tray in hand. The mirror reflected his image as he leaned over to set the tray on the table.

"Interesting decor," he murmured as he handed her a chunky white mug filled with soup. "Hope you like chicken noodle. It's salt free," he warned. "Carmichael said your sodium intake needed to be minimal."

Considering she'd just drunk nearly an entire glass of milk, she suspected she'd have eaten the soup, too, even if she didn't like it. "It's fine," she said truthfully.

In fact, she was suddenly starving, and it was all she could do not to attack the soup with him standing right there watching her. But as soon as he saw her scoop up a spoonful of slippery noodles, he went back to the kitchen.

A moment later, she heard him talking on his cell phone.

At least *that* was typical behavior for him. Alex and his cell phone had always been nearly surgically attached. The man was a serious workaholic.

Somewhat comforted by this small piece of normalcy, she devoured the soup. There was also a banana and two rolls on the tray, and she ate them, too.

Her gaze kept straying to the slice of kitchen she could see. Alex's voice was a low murmur, too indistinct for her to make out words. Given the coziness of the cabin, she knew he was deliberately keeping his voice low.

A personal call?

Alex was forty-two and the epitome of tall, dark and handsome. He was also extremely wealthy.

Women always flocked to him.

She brushed a bread crumb from her chest and leaned her head back against the arm of the couch. It was no business of hers whatsoever who Alex was speaking to.

Was it Valerie?

Still?

She closed her eyes. But while she could block out the sight of the cabin for lovers, she couldn't block out the low ebb and flow of Alex's voice. And she couldn't block out the thoroughly unwelcome fact that, while it was none of her business, she couldn't pretend that she didn't care.

She scooted down farther in the couch, wishing she could burrow beneath the red cushions and erase the past week.

Erase the past year, for that matter.

If she could, then Alex would still be the guy who changed women almost as often as he changed shirts. She'd still be working at his side, doing a job she really had loved, and keeping her own feelings for him sternly under wraps, because she was definitely too smart to think seriously about a man who sent nearly every woman off with some tasteful gift that *Nikki* had arranged for him.

If she could wish away the past year, Alex's ex-wife, Valerie, wouldn't have come back into his life, and Nikki wouldn't have had to quit her job because of her own foolish behavior.

She wouldn't be lying here now in this rabid honeymooner cabin, pregnant with the child of a man whose only appeal to her had been his strong resemblance to Alex.

Chapter Four

Alex couldn't sleep.

He couldn't blame it on the couch, though. It was comfortable enough, for a leather sectional large enough to host a cocktail party. No. It was the fact that he was listening for every sound that came from the massive bed on the other side of the fireplace.

He'd built a fire earlier that evening, but the logs had burned way down now. The only thing left of it was the warm scent and orange glow from the embers, which did nothing but illuminate the foot of the bed.

He wished the embers would die. Then he wouldn't be lying here peering through the firebox at the way the dark bedspread spilled partially off the rounded foot of the bed. It'd be better if Nikki would just kick it all the way off, he decided blearily. As it was, the velvety red fabric clinging tenuously to the mattress made him think of the way a woman's dress would cling to her shoulders as it was nudged off by her lover.

A woman?

He turned on his back, scrubbing his hands down his face.

Clearly, he'd been alone too damn long when he was thinking of his young former assistant in *that* way.

From the other side of the cabin, he heard a soft sigh. A rustle of bedding.

He slanted his gaze sideways.

Had the bedspread slid another perilous inch?

Annoyed, he swung his legs off the couch, knocking his ankle on the tacky coffee table. He cut off the none-too-quiet oath midsyllable.

What the hell was he doing here?

"Alex?" Nikki's voice was soft and husky from sleep. "Are you all right?"

His jaw tightened, along with every other part of him. "Yeah." It came out more of a grunt. Good to know his Ivy League education was so useful. He gingerly rotated his foot. "Are you? What's the matter?"

Again the rustling bedding.

God. He was something. The woman was having a crisis with her pregnancy and he was having visions of her peach-tinted skin draped in red velvet.

He should be asking what the *hell* was the matter with him.

"Nothing's wrong," she assured him. "You're the one who's over there swearing."

"You feeling more pain? Dizziness?"

"No." But she'd hesitated just a moment before answering. He reached over and grabbed his pants, hitching them up his hips as he rounded the fireplace.

There was a skylight above the bed, but the sky was so dark it didn't help illuminate the bedroom. There were only those orange embers casting their glow, softly enough for him to see the shape of her lying in the center of the round bed. "This isn't going to work if you're not honest about how you're feeling," he told her.

She moved, and the rustling sound made Alex feel as if something was brushing against *him*. He shook off the sensation and stepped closer. He could see the way the sheet draped over her knees. She'd sat up against a mound of pillows at the padded leather headboard.

Details he could've done without.

"Well?" he demanded.

She exhaled. "I don't lie." Her voice was tight.

Another few steps and he was at her bedside. He wasn't certain, but the sheets didn't look exactly white. More like silver. With a sheen.

He'd slept on five-hundred-dollar sheets that were smoother than silk, and five-dollar sheets that were as rough as sandpaper.

He'd never slept on satin sheets covering a round bed. There probably wasn't a single member of the Reed family who had.

You're not going to be the one to change that.

The voice inside his head was mocking.

"Okay. So you don't lie." Truth was, when she'd been in his employ, Nikki had been unfailingly honest, even when it meant tactfully telling him he was acting like an arrogant jerk. "But you can't hold back things, either."

Her hands flopped on the mattress and he realized she hadn't just drawn up her knees, she'd been hugging her leg. "I had a charley horse." Even husky from sleep, her voice managed to convey embarrassment.

He sat on the bed and stifled a sigh when she practically jumped six inches back. "Relax." He reached over and caught her leg through the sheet.

Satin. Definitely.

"What are you doing?"

"Where's the cramp?" His hand slid down her shin. Circled a very narrow ankle. He couldn't say he'd ever noticed before how delicately formed they were.

She'd usually been dressed from head to toe in very conservative, very tailored pantsuits.

She twisted her foot, trying to brush his hands aside. "It's gone now."

"And you wouldn't admit where it was if it weren't gone. It's not a crime to accept help, you know."

"I'm here, aren't I?"

"Yeah, but you don't want to be."

Her foot stopped moving. "And you *do?* Pull the other leg. It's got bells on."

He reached a little farther and caught the leg in question. "Nope. No bells ringing there." Just a cacophony of warning buzzers going off inside his head. He let go of her and stood. Shoved his hands in his pockets. "Is the bed comfortable, at least?"

"Yes. Except I feel like I might slide off the edge if I'm not careful. The sheets are pretty slippery. And I've, um, never slept on a round bed. It's a little…"

"Kinky?"

"Odd." Her voice sounded strangled. But she moved her feet again, and again he felt the sound like a physical thing. "I, um, I really could have taken the couch, you know. I didn't mind."

Shortly after lunch, he'd carried her from the couch to the bed, over her protests. "I'd mind."

She made a soft murmur that seemed distinctly female, and as such, was completely incapable of interpretation.

"Do you want some water or something?"

She reached out and picked up the glass he'd given her already. "Still full."

"Well, you should be drinking it," he murmured. Her arms were bare. When he'd put her to bed, she'd been wearing a long-sleeved sweater.

"If I were drinking glasses of water all night long, I'd be constantly going back and forth to the bathroom," she said huskily. "And since you've been dogged about carrying me there, too, you would get no more sleep than I would."

"Be glad the doctor said you didn't have to stay put so much that you needed a bedpan."

He couldn't see it, but he knew that she was blushing. Ornery bastard that he was, it made him smile.

"I'll drink it later," she assured him, holding up the sheet with the other hand. Making him wonder what she wore beneath it. He'd put her suitcase on a chair within reach of the bed. Presumably she'd had a nightgown in there or something.

"Let me know if the charley horse comes back."

"Fine."

"I mean it, Nikki."

"Or what? You'll fire me?" The tart comment seemed to surprise her as much as it did him. "I'll let you know." She slipped down to her side.

At the foot of the mattress, the bedspread gave up the ghost and sighed to the floor.

Alex's hands fisted inside his pockets. He returned to his side of the fireplace, but didn't bother lying down on the couch. He wasn't going to sleep.

He went into the kitchen and turned on the small light over the stove. At least here, there was a wall separating the space from the bedroom. The light shouldn't disturb Nikki.

He quietly carried an iron-backed bar stool from the minibar in the minuscule dining area and set it in the kitchen. His briefcase was already open on the counter next to the toaster, and he pulled out a stack of papers and envelopes—mail that he'd grabbed on his way out the door to the airport days ago and still hadn't read— and dumped everything on the counter.

Then he poured himself a small measure of bourbon in one of the plentiful glasses the cabin was stocked with.

He sat down, propped his elbows on the counter and swirled the liquor gently in the glass.

The other advantage of the wall between the kitchen and bedroom was that *he* couldn't waste any time wondering how long it'd be before a damn bedspread fell off a damn mattress.

He tossed back half the contents of the glass and set it aside. Too bad he didn't have a handy wall inside his head, cordoning off the question that had been squatting there.

What kind of man could capture Nikki's attention deeply enough to leave her pregnant?

And why the hell wasn't the guy *with* her?

The heavenly smell of coffee woke Nikki the following morning. She didn't even open her eyes at first. Just lay there still as a mouse, cradled in a soft jumble of pillows, as she slowly breathed in that wonderful, wonderful aroma.

Oh, what she wouldn't give for a good dose of caffeine-rich coffee. But all caffeinated drinks and any foods that were remotely salty—and therefore flavorful—were now stricken from her allowable list.

So she lay there and savored the smell, and pretended not to notice that she was practically salivating all the while.

But lying there like a bump could only last so long before her back started to ache, so she turned over, stretching out her legs, pointing her toes. When she'd first seen the silver satin sheets, she'd been somewhat appalled. But the fact was, they felt pretty darn nice. Slippery, true. But nice.

So she swished her legs lazily over them a few more times, her head still buried in the pillow.

"I had a dog once who chased rabbits in his sleep."

Nikki froze at the amused comment. The cool satin warmed beneath her still legs.

"Corkscrew would be nearly snoring, but his legs would be going a mile a minute. That's what you remind me of."

Since the earth wasn't likely to mercifully swallow her whole anytime soon, she lifted her head out of the pillow and eyed Alex. "A dog named Corkscrew. How…flattering." And trust Alex, the wine connoisseur, to have had a dog named Corkscrew. "What happened to him?"

"Died of old age. Now he's chasing rabbits for eternity."

She pushed her hair out of her face and propped her head on her hand. Looking at Alex was dangerous, but she couldn't very well avoid doing so for the next few weeks.

He hadn't shaved, but his wet hair was ruthlessly combed back from his face. He'd obviously showered, and the fact that she'd slept right through it gave her a moment's unease.

She'd never lived with anyone. Not that she was *living* with Alex, of course. But she'd have thought she'd be more aware of sounds around her that weren't made by, well, *her.*

He was wearing a thick, ivory fisherman's sweater, which made his shoulders look about a mile wide. That wasn't so odd in itself. Nor was it odd that he was un-shaven. There'd been plenty of times when he'd worked all night and in the morning would pull out his electric razor, running it brusquely over his lean cheeks while they'd gone through the upcoming day's business.

What was odd was that he was wearing blue jeans. Well-worn jeans, in fact. So worn they were nearly white in certain places. A person could purchase jeans in that condition these days, but Nikki had one stepfa-ther, five stepbrothers and a brother-in-law whose jeans all looked remarkably similar, so she recognized the real deal when she saw them.

She wouldn't have expected Alex to have a pair so broken in. Maybe he'd hired the task out to someone. A surrogate jeans breaker-in-er.

Good grief, did she ever need caffeine.

"Last one I ever had," he mused, lifting his mug of that wonderful-smelling stuff to his mouth.

She moistened her lips. Was it the coffee that had her mouth watering, or was it the man drinking it? "Last what?"

His eyes crinkled a little at the corners. "Dog."

She felt her cheeks heat. Corkscrew. "Right. I never knew you had a dog."

"That's because I was nine."

She sat up a little more. She had a hard time envision-ing Alex as a boy. "Why didn't you get another dog?"

He shrugged. "Went away to boarding school. No point in having a dog if you're not around to give it some attention."

She felt as if she'd learned more about Alex in the last two minutes than she had in years. "Was your school far away from home?"

"An hour or so."

The baby shifted when she tucked a pillow beneath her knees under the sheet. "Did you go home on weekends?"

"Rarely. How do you want your eggs?"

"Emily, one of my sisters-in-law, went to boarding school when she was a teenager. But it was back east somewhere, I think. She says she hated it."

"Some people do. Over easy or scrambled?"

"I'm not sure how I feel about you cooking for me."

"Scrambled it is."

Her lips parted as he turned away. She saw his legs through the fireplace when he walked through the living area on the other side. Then she couldn't see him anymore, but could hear him in the kitchen. Opening cupboards. Rattling pans.

"Over easy," she called after him. "Thank you."

She heard his cell phone beep and then his low voice. "Hi, babe."

Great. If it wasn't Valerie, it could have been any other dozen women he was addressing. She didn't want to overhear another word, and she started to swing her legs off the bed, intending to go to the bathroom.

The tips of her toes were engulfed in shaggy animal-print carpet before she stopped. She slowly drew back her feet until they rested on the mattress, and her knees would have been under her chin if not for the bulge of the baby.

She wasn't supposed to walk anywhere. How could she forget that? Just because Alex was talking to his latest squeeze?

She pushed both hands against her temples, then raked back her hair, holding it behind her neck, and studied her reflection in the mirrored wall opposite the bed. The football jersey she wore was old, the once-deep red now faded to a milky, tomato soup color.

It had been Cody's.

For a while, when she'd learned she was pregnant, she had stopped wearing the shirt to bed. Feeling as if continuing to wear it would be a betrayal of him, somehow. But when she'd lain awake night after night, she'd finally dug it out of her drawer and put it on.

Her sleep had improved, but only marginally.

"Want toast?" Alex asked loudly.

"Yes." She wondered if he cooked breakfast for his female guests.

Doubtful. She'd arranged a few dinner meetings for him at the Echelon. Alex need only express a request and the staff there hopped. The breakfast, tastefully arranged on sterling, dome-covered platters, would arrive on a linen-draped cart. Like something out of a movie.

She lowered her forehead to her knees and closed her eyes. Her fingers absently worked through the tangles in her hair.

Speculating over who Alex shared breakfast with had never particularly pained her. Not until he'd broken his own record of loving and leaving them within a few weeks by continuing to see Valerie for *months*. On end.

That had hurt. Seeing his smile whenever Valerie dropped by for an unexpected visit—during which he always shut his office door. Normally, Alex *never* shut the door between his office and Nikki's. Not even when he was firing someone.

"Here. You got scrambled, anyway. Yolks broke when I cracked the shells."

She looked up to see Alex holding out a plate. Along with the eggs, there was toast. Cut in half diagonally and a little too brown beneath the red jam, but she was too hungry to complain.

"Thanks." She started to take the plate, but he held it out of reach.

"Scoot back."

She lowered her legs, flushing a little because Cody's shirt was falling off one shoulder and the hem ended midthigh. She slid back on the bed, swiftly pulling the slippery silver sheet over herself as she did so. When Alex finally handed her the plate, his eyes were full of amusement.

So she didn't look at his eyes. She focused on the plate. Before she could set it on her lap, though, he whipped a red-and-blue-checked dish towel over her thighs. "Wouldn't want to get strawberry jam on the sheets," he murmured.

Without thought, Nikki snorted softly. "A little strawberry jam is probably the most innocent thing this room has seen on the sheets." She was cringing before the last word left her lips, and she shoved half a toast slice in her mouth to confiscate the jam.

Alex had an unholy grin on his face when she finally was able to swallow. But he said nothing. Just handed her the tall glass of milk he held.

She took a sip and set it aside on the nightstand, then started on the eggs. "They're pretty good."

"Imagine that."

She took another forkful, glancing up at him. "Aren't you going to eat?"

"Already did."

"You, um, don't have to stay here to keep me company while I eat. You must have things you need to do."

"Watching the ficus grow?"

She felt her face flushing. "Calls. Huffington business. I still can't imagine how you've stood being away from the office this long."

"Calling me a workaholic?"

"Not in a bad way."

His eyes narrowed a little as if he found that tidbit interesting. In fact, he was looking at her as if he found her interesting. Like a…financial report he was perusing, or something.

She shoved a last forkful of fluffy eggs in her mouth and hurriedly swallowed. She grabbed the other slice of toast and handed the plate back to him, hoping he'd take it and go, and stop watching her that way with those dark eyes.

"You didn't finish your eggs."

"I'm full."

He exhaled. Shook his head and set the plate on the nightstand alongside the milk. "Finish. And don't hide those eggs under the pillow, either," he warned. "When you're done I'll carry you to the bathroom."

Another mortifying coin to add to her purse of memories.

She waited until he'd rounded the fireplace again before she chomped through her toast and finished the eggs. The milk was a little harder going down. If there had been a potted plant within reach, she would have strongly considered dumping some there.

And even though she'd have dearly loved to put off having to prevail upon him again, she was at the mercy of her pregnant body. "Okay. I'm done," she called out finally. She knew she sounded as cranky as a two-year-old, but couldn't seem to stop it.

She glared at his legs through the fireplace when he passed by again.

Alex didn't comment on her expression, since she could see, courtesy of the mirror across from her, that it was very much still in place when he stopped next to the bed. "Do you need anything from your suitcase?"

"If you wouldn't mind setting the whole thing in the bathroom, I'll pull out what I need."

It took him all of two seconds to do that, then he leaned down and slid his hands beneath her.

It was as startling as it had been every other time he'd carried her, and she closed her hands nervously over his shoulders as he straightened. "You're going to regret this before long," she said. "Should have rented a crane to heft me around."

His hands tightened a little as he turned.

And there was their reflection in that dratted mirror. It wasn't even a plain old mirror. Of course not. Not in this place. The thing was bordered by etched engravings that in the light of day were clearly entwined bodies.

Then Alex was moving, carrying her past the mirror and setting her on the closed lid of the commode. Before he shut the door, giving her privacy at last, his gaze skipped over the interior of the bathroom.

More mirrors.

"This place is something else, isn't it?"

Nikki nodded, but he was already gone.

She sighed. Looked at the multitude of reflections. It wasn't the place that kept putting impossible thoughts in her head.

It was the man.

Chapter Five

One day down. How many more to go?

Alex rinsed the soap from the last glass and stuck it upside down in the plastic rack next to the sink. It barely fit alongside the rest of the dishes they'd used that day. He turned off the faucet, dried his hands on his thighs and looked at the stack of work that had arrived by courier a few hours earlier. He'd moved it—as well as all his other papers—away from the stove, to keep from spilling anything on them, but other than that, he'd accomplished little work besides opening the courier pouch to glance through what was inside.

It wasn't Nikki's fault that he'd gotten little accomplished. She'd pretty much worn herself out just using the shower, where he'd placed a sturdy seat so she could bathe without standing. When she'd called to him that she was finished, she'd been pale and tired, the tart woman clearly tucked away for a while. He'd set her back on the bed, which he'd straightened while she'd bathed, and she'd promptly rolled on her side, presenting him with the back side of her jeans and deep blue sweater.

A back side, from the thick rope of her wet hair that began at her nape and ended at the middle of her spine, that looked surprisingly narrow for a woman carrying a soccer ball in the front.

Fortunately, she'd spent most of the day napping, blissfully unaware of Alex's apparent dive into lecherousness. She'd wakened barely long enough to eat lunch and dinner. Now, he figured, she'd sleep the night through.

He pulled up the bar stool to the counter. Instead of pouring a glass of bourbon this time, he leaned over and punched the button on the coffeemaker. In seconds, a narrow stream of coffee began pouring into the glass carafe. Too impatient to wait for the pot to fill, he pushed the carafe aside and stuck his mug beneath the stream instead. Several drops hit the hot base and hissed, spitting and bubbling. As soon as his mug was full, he shoved the carafe back in place and turned to the mess of reports and correspondence spilling out of the pouch.

After firing his latest assistant, he'd grabbed Miriam, the senior staff member in his payroll department, and told her she was responsible for his office until he found someone else. She'd obviously just collected everything that had come across his desk and forwarded it without even attempting to handle any minor matters herself.

He'd already opened and read through the one letter that had leaped out at him simply by virtue of the return address.

Trust his family to send a cool letter on engraved RHS letterhead warning that not only had they not given up their investigation into adding Huffington Sports Clinics to their holdings, but they were stepping up their efforts. The matter would be voted on at the next board meeting. If it passed, RHS would take steps to acquire his company. One way or the other.

They shouldn't have had a chance in hell, of course. Alex had told his father that when the matter arose months earlier. No damn way. Huffington was privately held. By him.

Maybe his clinics—despite their innovativeness—*had* become successful enough to have drawn the eye of his staunchly conservative family. But in the scheme of things, his shop was small potatoes compared to RHS.

It wasn't *business* that was motivating the chairman of the board of RHS. His father. Alex Reed, Sr. The bane of Alex's existence. It was personal. Alex was becoming too successful in his own right, so it was time for his father to shut him down. Teach him a lesson.

Just as he'd warned when Alex left the family's suffocating "fold" more than twenty years earlier. Didn't matter that so much time had passed. His father was a patient man, and he never forgot a promise, even one of ruination.

On the good side, the only maneuvering power RHS had over Alex was in blocking his current attempts for expansion through some acquisitions of his own. Macfield Technologies, specialists in equipment design and manufacturing, combined with Huffington's existing stronghold in sports medicine, would position him well through the next few decades.

Without Macfield?

Competing with the major health systems, like RHS, that were finally getting on board with newer thinking in the field of sports medicine, would be nigh impossible for Huffington within the next few years.

Alex needed Macfield. And Macfield desperately needed an infusion of capital. If RHS beat Alex to that particular punch, he might as well sell out to them, too.

The thought was intolerable. He'd rather sell the company he'd founded off to the lowest bidder than see it be swallowed whole by the Reed family empire.

He rubbed his forehead, staring at the latest missive from RHS.

There was only one way his old man could have learned about Alex's interest in Macfield. Alex had mentioned it to Val nearly a year earlier, when he'd first started courting standoffish George Macfield. And despite her intention to stay away from his cousin, Hunter, she probably hadn't. Not when he'd shown up in Cheyenne last summer. Val had never kept secrets well from Hunt. And Hunt…well, Alex's cousin had never been good at keeping secrets from the family.

"Alex?" Nikki's voice was soft. Faint.

Alarm propelled him into the dim bedroom. "What's wrong?" She was propped up on one hand. She'd undone her braid and her hair flowed in a dark shadow over her shoulder.

"I'm sorry. I just need to use the bathroom."

He realized he'd carried in both his coffee mug and the letter. He exhaled and set them both on the nightstand. "Don't be sorry." He'd have another twenty dozen gray hairs to add to the ones he already possessed from the adrenaline rush that was barely subsiding, but he'd live. He leaned over and picked her up.

Another jolt ripped through him when her hair rippled over his arm.

It was softer than he expected. He quickly carried her into the bathroom and deposited her on the small padded bench next to the vanity. In the light of the bathroom she looked wan. "Are you sure you're feeling okay?"

She was staring fixedly at the floor. "Give me a few minutes."

Her embarrassment was palpable. He stepped outside, pulling the door closed.

A moment later he heard the faucet running, and he retrieved his father's letter and the coffee and put them back in the kitchen. But a soft, distinctive sound made him spin on his heel.

He didn't bother knocking on the door.

He just pushed it open.

And there she sat, hunched over the commode, wretching.

"Jesus," he muttered, ignoring the teary look she shot

him before she hastily turned away. He grabbed a wash-cloth off the stack piled on a glass shelf built into the mirrored wall, and wet it.

"Go away," she begged. "Please."

He ignored that, too, and pulled the bench closer, to sit on the end of it. He reached out to grab her hair back and handed her the wet cloth. Irritation coated his concern. "Shut up, Nik."

She flushed the toilet and buried her face in the cloth, her nausea apparently abating for the moment. "You're the only person besides Belle who's ever called me that." Her voice was muffled.

His knuckles grazed the knitted collar of her sweater. It was soft. But her hair was softer. Her legs were folded beneath her, and she looked painfully small curled miserably on the floor the way she was.

"If you want your sister here," he promised quietly, "I'll find her."

"She's on her honeymoon."

"You think she'd rather not know about this?" He smoothed his hand down her hair, combing his fingers through it.

She sighed, seeming to lean her head back into his touch for a moment. But then she must have realized it, for she put a few inches between them. She lowered the cloth and bunched it in her fist. Her neck drooped tiredly, like some flower stem under a heavy bloom. "Why are you being so nice, Alex?"

His pause was infinitesimal. "I'm a nice guy."

She shook her head a little and the motion worked

its way down to where his fingers were still entwined in her hair. "No. You're not. You're a lot of things, but nice just for the sake of it has never been one of them."

"Suppose anyone would feel that way if I'd fired their sister."

"You didn't fire Belle. You put her on a leave of absence." An enormous sigh lifted Nikki's shoulders, only to leave her drooping even more. "And if you hadn't, she wouldn't have gone to work for Cage and they wouldn't be on their honeymoon right now."

Alex was glad things had worked out well for Belle. "I'd have rather fired Scott Langtree. The guy was slime."

"Can't fire a patient," Nikki murmured. "He proposed to her, you know. Convinced her that he was free to marry. Until his wife showed up, my sister believed him."

Alex eyed Nikki's locks. Under the overhead light, he could see glints of gold among the red.

Another thing he hadn't noticed before.

"She didn't tell me that."

"She was humiliated enough to have fallen for his line. Why would she have told you that when you'd called her on the carpet for becoming personally involved with one of her own therapy cases? She knew she shouldn't have gotten involved in the first place, whether or not he was still married."

Langtree's affair with one of Huffington's junior physical therapists had caused a minor furor. Particularly when Langtree's wife got vocal in the media about her football player husband's behavior. Huffington didn't need that kind of reputation, and Alex had been forced to act on it. "You were angry with me for censuring Belle."

"Everyone who works at Huffington knows the rule against fraternizing. Among staff and patients."

"You sound like you're quoting the personnel policy manual." His hand had reached the ends of her hair, and the locks curled around his fingers. "Is that why you quit? Because you were mad about it?" More than half a year had passed by then, though.

"I was angry with the Langtrees. I was hurt for Belle, because she really had thought she cared about him. And, no, that is not why I resigned." Nikki stretched her hand out to set the cloth on the sink.

"Feeling better?"

She nodded.

"Does this happen often?"

"Not anymore." She pressed her hand over her forehead. "I had pretty bad morning sickness early on."

He remembered how sick Valerie had been before she'd lost the baby. "Maybe we should call the doctor."

"No. No. I'm fine. Really." Nikki dropped her hand and looked up at him, as if to convince him of the truth of it. "I'm feeling better already. Truly."

"Hmm. Well, next time just say you're going to hurl."

Her eyes, as deep a blue as the sweater she wore, slanted up at him, vaguely shocked. Her lashes were tipped with the same gold glints that shone in her hair. "I wouldn't have thought that 'hurl' was even in your vocabulary."

"Ivy Leaguers throw keg parties, too."

Her brows rose. She suddenly tilted her head, sniffing suspiciously. "Have you been drinking now? Or are you teasing me?"

If his nerves were a little more unknotted, he'd have been amused. "Neither."

"Are you sure?"

"Believe me. I'd know." He stood, shoving the bench back as he stood. "Ready to go back to bed?"

"I want to brush my teeth."

He dragged the bench forward again until it was situated in front of the sink. He ignored her frown and lifted her onto it.

"I could have managed that."

"Yeah. I know. You're the original independent woman. Never need a man for anything." He handed her the pink toothbrush that was upended in the clear glass on the sink next to his white one, and turned on the water for her. "Except that." He flattened his palm briefly against the bulge of her abdomen. "Don't think you did that without a man. Speaking of whom, where the hell is he?"

Her fingers tightened on the tube of toothpaste, squirting out twice what the toothbrush could hold. "I beg your pardon?" She shoved the toothbrush in her mouth, swishing it violently over her teeth.

"Can't quite see you going to a sperm bank." Anger stirred inside him, out of nowhere. "But then again, maybe that would be right up your alley. Decide to have a kid, but don't want to actually have to involve someone else in the process."

She leaned forward and spat. Rinsed her mouth with water and shoved the toothbrush back into the glass, where it rattled against his. "You don't know what you're talking about."

"So tell me."

"Why? What possible reason could any of it matter to you? I don't work for you anymore! So if you're afraid it was someone who worked at Huffington, or a patient, get over it." She started to push herself off the bench, as if she wanted nothing more than to get away from him, but froze midway.

She subsided slowly on the padded seat. She didn't look at him, but courtesy of the mirrors surrounding them, he could see the glitter of tears in her eyes.

She'd mentioned the father not being involved with Huffington. Why?

"Does the father know?"

She lifted her hands in a futile gesture. "Yes."

"And?"

"And what? He's not involved. Believe me."

Too emphatic, he thought. And didn't like the fact that it bothered him. A lot. "Do you love him?"

Her lips parted. "No!"

"Yet you slept with him."

A flood of color rose above the high collar of her sweater and crept up into her cheeks. "Be careful, Alex," she said after a moment, her voice soft and shaking. "Or you'll be sounding hypocritical. I don't believe you're in love with every woman who has gotten friendly with your bedsheets. And since I was usually charged with sending them off with their parting piece of jewelry—" her voice got tighter "—I have some sense of how many there were before Valerie reappeared."

"Yeah, but that's me."

"And you're so great that you get to have a different standard?"

"No. You are."

Her lips parted, but nothing came out. Naked vulnerability shone in her blue eyes. "Don't assume that you know me."

"I guess I figured that out when you left me for no good reason." The words held a connotation that wasn't applicable to the situation. But he didn't retract them. Didn't correct them.

Nor did she.

Silence ticked between them, and it might just as well have bounced off the mirrors because of the way it thickened. Tightened.

A tear slid down her cheek.

His jaw was so tight it ached, and he consciously relaxed. It wasn't Nikki causing his tension. It was the situation with RHS and Macfield.

Had to be.

He leaned down to pick her up.

She shied away and he froze. "Gonna spend the night here in the bathroom?"

"Maybe." Her voice was tight. "Maybe I'd rather crawl back to bed than be carried again."

Only her condition kept him from grabbing her and tossing her over his shoulder. And the fact that he had to struggle not to do just that shook him. "You're a *very* stubborn woman."

"Then you must be relieved not to have me in your office!"

He walked out of the bathroom, leaving her sitting there.

She wanted to crawl? She could crawl.

He went into the kitchen. The carafe was nearly full of coffee. The courier pouch hadn't moved. His father's letter was still sitting on top of the stack of memos that Miriam had forwarded.

He rubbed his hand down his face.

Let out a long breath and returned to the bathroom.

Nikki hadn't moved.

He silently picked her up and carried her back to the bed.

She didn't argue. And when he leaned over, still holding her, and whipped back the velvet spread before setting her in the center of all that silver satin, she murmured a quiet, polite, "Thank you."

"Do you need anything else?"

Her gaze slanted to the nightstand. And even though it was well within her reach, he pulled open the single drawer. A neatly folded jersey was the only thing inside, and he lifted it out, dropping it on the bed beside her.

Her fingers closed over it, drawing it over her lap in a motion that struck him as protective. She murmured another killingly polite thanks.

He nodded and rounded the fireplace, skirting the

couch and the heart-shaped tub. The kitchen and all of his problems spread on the counter there waited for him.

He grabbed his coat off the hook and let himself out the front door instead.

It was a clear, dark night. The moon was just beginning to climb above the tall pines on the horizon, and the light from it gleamed on the snow.

Appreciating the view was not something he could do just then.

It was a helluva note to realize that he preferred Nikki's temper over the politeness.

When she heard the door close, Nikki turned on her side and slowly lowered herself against the pillows, clutching the shirt to her chest. Neither she nor Alex had shut off the light in the bathroom, and it shone brightly into the bedroom.

She turned on her other side, away from the light.

It would serve her right if he got in his vehicle and left her here to fend for herself. What did he owe her, after all?

Not a single thing.

And she still couldn't fathom what had prompted any of his actions, anyway. She had been good at her job, but so were any number of qualified people.

When the door didn't sound again, signaling Alex's return—and down deep she knew he would return—she finally sat up and slid out of her jeans and turtleneck. Every muscle inside her screamed for sleep, as badly as she'd craved sleep in the first weeks of her pregnancy.

She dropped the clothes on the floor beside the bed, not even bothering to fold them. She tugged off her bra and felt nothing but relief because the thing had been growing increasingly tight the past few weeks. She needed some new clothes. Up to now she'd managed mostly with oversize sweaters and the few maternity pants and jeans she'd bought. But she wouldn't be able to scrape by like this much longer.

If she didn't earn some money soon to buy more, she'd end up going on a shopping spree with her mother, who would simply insist on it.

Not that Nikki didn't enjoy her mother's company. She did. But she had stopped allowing her mom to outfit her wardrobe when she was a teenager, and the habit was ingrained.

She tugged the jersey over her head and lay back again, pulling up the sheet. Yet as sleepy as she was, as bone-deep tired as she felt, she didn't fall asleep.

If you want your sister here, I'll find her.

She believed him. And she struggled against the temptation: She and Belle had never lived in each other's hip pockets. They'd have driven each other mad if they had. But Nikki couldn't ever recall missing her twin as much as she did now.

Not even after Cody died.

But what would she say to Belle if she were here? Would she tell her sister, finally, the monumentally foolish details of how she'd ended up in her condition?

That, depressed not only over Alex's evidently renewed relationship with his ex-wife, but at the passing of another year marking the anniversary of Cody's death, she'd let herself be seduced by a man who looked remarkably like Alex, yet wasn't?

She'd met Alex's cousin on only three occasions. The first time, he'd walked into her office, propped a hip on her desk and grinned a ridiculously charming grin that hadn't moved her in the least.

It wasn't Hunter Reed's gregarious, flirtatious nature that had seduced her.

It was the fact that he looked uncannily like Alex.

But Hunter Reed was most definitely *not* Alex. And when she'd felt honor-bound to notify him about the pregnancy resulting from that one miserable night, he'd let her know in no uncertain terms that he was not going to be held responsible for her brat.

He'd sent an exorbitant check, along with a ream of legal documents to that effect, in return for leaving him alone.

She'd tossed the check and the documents in a box deep in a closet, and been grateful that she wouldn't ever have to deal with any member of the Reed family again.

Nikki heard the door open and close. Alex was back.

So much for that belief.

Chapter Six

Five days down, too many to go.

Nikki flipped three more playing cards down on the bed beside her. She'd been playing solitaire for only a few minutes, but it felt as if she'd been at it for hours.

Days.

She sighed and glanced over at the television. She had the sound nearly muted. She was tired of listening to endless weather reports of a storm that was supposed to blow in sometime that day.

She wasn't worried about a storm. Alex had cut enough wood to last through the millennium.

He was currently in the kitchen, where she couldn't see him, but could hear the cadence of his voice.

He was angry and making no attempt to hide it.

A courier had delivered another fat package late that afternoon while she was eating a peanut butter sandwich. Alex had been out back near the shed that was visible from one of the windows next to the bed. He'd been chopping wood, and she'd been paying far more attention to the sight of him than she had to the lunch he'd prepared for her.

Who knew that Alex could wield an ax with a wicked swing when he felt compelled to do so?

When the courier truck had lumbered into view, he'd strode past her windows, the ax propped over his shoulder to sign for the package, and she'd quickly tended to the lunch rather than have him come in and see how little she'd eaten. He would want to know if she was feeling poorly again, and she didn't want to lie about that. Mostly, she wouldn't want to admit she'd been ogling him.

Now there was a mammoth quantity of split logs stacked near the fireplace, and he was inside again. Slamming cupboard doors every now and then, particularly when his voice rose. Which it had been doing more and more of late.

Since the night he'd barged in on her and demanded to know where the father of her child was—if there even *was* a father—they'd both gone out of their way to avoid personal matters.

As much as could be avoided, given the situation.

But such careful behavior was a stress all on its own, one that was driving her quietly out of her mind.

She slapped the queen of hearts under the king of clubs and pitied Miriam Delmar, who seemed to be the focus of Alex's latest frustration. Nikki was on the verge of begging him to stop yelling at Miriam, when she heard a crash and an oath.

Her hands scattered the solitaire game as she sat up. "Alex? You okay?"

More clattering. More cursing. Then belatedly, "Yeah. Fine."

A little information, please? She waited, but none seemed forthcoming. "What happened?"

"Dropped the cell phone in the frickin' dishwater and tipped over the bar stool."

She clapped her hand over her mouth to muffle the laughter that sneaked up on her.

Another oath came from him. "Are you laughing in there?"

"Ah…no," she managed to reply. She barely had time to school her expression before she saw his legs through the fireplace and he entered the room.

"Funny?" He held up his small cell phone. Soapsuds were still clinging to it, and water dripped down his forearm where he'd shoved up the sleeve of his dark gray sweater. "This place doesn't even have a damn landline."

She bit her lip, but her shoulders shook a little with suppressed laughter. She leaned over to the nightstand, which had slowly but surely been filling up with her personal items since they'd arrived. She unearthed her own cell phone from beneath the edge of a decorating magazine she'd found on a shelf in the bathroom. "Here." She extended it to him. "You can use mine."

He walked closer. Started to reach for it, but she

yanked it back out of his grasp. "Wait. One condition," she warned.

He raised a dark, slashing eyebrow. "Condition?"

"Barking at Miriam isn't going to make her more productive. She's always been terrified of you."

The brow lowered, joining the other. "Barking." His voice was mild.

"Yes. Barking. She's probably scrambling to keep things on an even keel with you gone, but I'm sure she's doing her best, and—"

"She's sending me crap that any reasonably intelligent secretary should be able to handle on her own!"

"But she's not your secretary. She's not *anyone's* secretary. She's the head payroll clerk!"

He exhaled sharply. "Then you call her and tell her to get a cell phone to me in tomorrow's courier pouch. At least *that* will be something useful she can do."

He looked so utterly aggravated, and so out of character with his cashmere sweater splashed by soapsuds and water, that Nikki felt as much sympathy for him as she did poor Miriam.

And she was bored out of her skull because of her enforced inactivity. Boredom that allowed her mind to trip down roads it had no business traveling. "Fine. I'll talk to her."

His eyes sharpened. "You will?"

She nodded. "And you might as well bring me the courier pouch. Maybe I can take care of some of the routine stuff for you and you can…relax a little."

He snorted, because they both knew he rarely relaxed. "Sure you want to do that? Might smack a little of working for me again."

"Consider it returning the favor," she murmured, with far more blitheness than she felt. "For everything you've been doing for me. But that's all it is. A favor. I'm not coming back to work for you."

"I didn't ask you to," he reminded her.

"Not recently," she allowed.

But he was smiling a little. And she knew better than to trust that faint, corner-of-the-mouth-tilted-upward smile. "I mean it, Alex. I am not coming back to Huffington." It had taken every bit of strength she'd possessed to leave in the first place. She couldn't let herself backslide *now*.

The baby kicked.

It felt like agreement to Nikki.

"Don't get yourself worked up about it," he said, which didn't convince her at all that he took her assurance seriously. He left long enough to retrieve the courier pouch, which he dumped on the bed beside her. "And speaking of getting worked up. You're not to overdo it."

As she reached for the pouch, there was an undeniable wave of anticipation building inside her that she hoped to heaven was not apparent to him. "How on earth can I overdo something when I'm lying down every hour of the day?" She slid out a massive amount of interoffice envelopes, correspondence and reports, and tossed the pouch aside. She understood his frustration when she immediately noticed the quantity of junk mail that Miriam had sent.

"Don't forget the replacement cell phone."

Her fingers were already busy, nimbly sorting and prioritizing. "I won't forget. Oh, my." She paused. "Miriam must have stuck this in by mistake. It's your personal calendar from last year. Had you asked her for your current one?"

"No." He held out his hand, and her fingers grazed his when she handed the thick book to him.

He flipped it open. Fanned through the pages.

Her hand curled at her side. "You, um, well, she should definitely stick that back in your files. You never know when you might need to go back and check the dates of a meeting or something." Alex was very technologically minded, but he was old-fashioned when it came to keeping his calendar.

She'd always thought it was kind of cute.

But when she eyed him, his smile was tight.

"I'll call Miriam first thing in the morning," she reiterated quickly.

"Thank you. Now, may I still use your phone?"

"Oh. Right." She held it out and his hand brushed hers once more as he took it.

She curled her fingers against her palm, but the tingling remained.

After a moment, he turned to leave the bedroom. Nikki watched him in the mirror, only to flush when his gaze captured hers in the reflection.

"Don't overdo it," he reminded her, not breaking his stride.

She looked down at her belly. "Hear that?" she whispered. "Mr. Reed has spoken."

"Mr. Reed has good hearing."

She started. Alex was crouched on the opposite side of the fireplace, looking through at her. He set another log in place, then scratched one of the long matches from the metal container—there were identical ones on each side of the fireplace—and set the flame to the kindling.

The tiny blaze wavered, then licked. Caught. Spread. And still Alex watched her.

The warmth from the fireplace was immediate. Or maybe it was warmth coming from inside her.

She dragged her gaze away from his and blindly reached for the courier pouch again, to pull out another handful.

When she finally had the nerve to look up again, Alex was gone.

Her fingers went lax, and the invitations to events, dinners, conferences fell to the mattress. She swallowed. Closed her eyes for a moment, gathering herself.

After a while, her heart stopped pounding in her ears, and she could hear Alex talking again, this time on her cell phone. His voice wasn't raised, which didn't necessarily mean a thing.

But sitting here wondering if it was business he was discussing, or if it was a personal matter—Valerie?—was too disturbing. Nikki leaned over, unearthed a pen from the cluttered nightstand and started writing notes to Miriam on the most glaringly important items.

* * *

He shouldn't have put the courier pouch within ten feet of her slender hands, Alex thought later that night as he watched the foot of the bed again through the flames flickering in the fireplace. He'd left her poring over the contents, and when he'd checked on her again, she'd fallen asleep with her cheek against a press release for the Valentine's Day dance Huffington sponsored every year benefiting various charities. The dance wasn't for another month, but his marketing department was gearing up for the good PR that the event garnered each year.

Nikki had slept right through dinner. Hadn't stirred when he crouched beside the bed and quietly spoke her name. Had done nothing but sigh a little and turn more fully toward him when he'd done the monumentally stupid thing of brushing her hair away from her cheek.

He should never have touched her hair. Not that night in the bathroom when she'd lost her cookies. Not tonight when she'd been sound asleep on a pile of papers that he paid *staff* to handle.

At least she was sleeping, though, and not leaning over the toilet losing her lunch.

He held up the cell phone he'd been using since she'd loaned it to him, and hit Redial. Valerie's voice mail at the Echelon was, again, the only answer he got.

God knew where his ex-wife was these days. She'd been out every evening when he'd called, ever since he'd come to Montana. She'd gotten herself more under control since she'd shown up nearly a year earlier in Cheyenne, desperately upset over another episode with Hunt. She'd stuck with AA for longer than she'd ever managed before. And—as long as she kept passing the drug tests she'd agreed to—she was doing a decent enough job handling PR for Huffington's philanthropic interests. She was on the ball at least when it came to the Valentine's Day dance.

She was probably out at a meeting.

Alex hoped.

The last thing he needed was Val taking a nosedive again. Aside from the time he gave to Huffington, he'd spent more time saving her from herself than anything else in his life.

He'd known he was taking a chance on being gone this long. But he'd needed to do something where Val was concerned. She'd been getting too attached to him lately. He'd support her in most any way he could, because they went back so far, but he wasn't about to be a substitute for Hunter. Not again. He wanted her to stand on her *own* feet for once.

Trouble was, unless she'd answer her phone, he was left wondering whether his absence helped the situation or had her backsliding all over again.

He tossed aside the cell phone, then jabbed the poker into the fire a few times before putting the screen in place on both sides of the fireplace.

Then he looked through the flames at Nikki. He'd already moved aside the mess of papers and envelopes, and pulled the velvet spread over her legs.

She was about as different from Val as a woman

could get. Val of the blond hair and killing smile who'd needed him would never understand the independence that drove Nikki. She'd considered it her due to accept help. Nikki did so in order not to interrupt her sister's honeymoon or her mother's vacation.

He turned off the lamp next to the red couch and peeled down to his shorts and T-shirt. Then he grabbed the quilt that he'd been using as bedding, and stretched out. Tomorrow he'd have his new cell phone, he'd handle the conference call with the boys at Macfield, which had taken him too bloody long to arrange, and he'd tell his human resources department to pull in an administrative assistant from one of the other sites.

He'd pay the person whatever it took to get him or her to Cheyenne. Even though *he* was loyal to the town and his flagship clinic, he knew it wasn't always an enticing prospect for someone living in a major metropolitan area—where his other sites were located. Money, though, had a way of overriding such details.

He threw his arm over his eyes. Outside the cabin, the wind picked up, whistling through the eaves, gusting down the chimney to make the flames spit and dance. The storm the news had been predicting all day had evidently arrived.

Suited him just fine.

He couldn't go around rattling windows and screaming through trees.

Sleep wasn't coming any easier tonight than it had since they'd arrived, though, and he finally found the remote for the television and flicked it on, keeping the sound low so it wouldn't disturb Nikki. The cabin didn't come with a phone line, but it came with satellite television.

Go figure.

He found a sports channel and tossed aside the remote. The leather creaked as he lay back on the couch. But the sports recap didn't hold his attention the way he'd hoped, because he kept looking through the flames at the bed.

Far as he could tell, Nikki hadn't moved a muscle.

He exhaled roughly and finally rose, going to check on her. He turned the light on in the bathroom so he could see better, but pulled the door nearly shut so it wouldn't disturb her.

She was curled in a knot, one arm flung wide, palm upward, fingers curled slightly. Her breathing was soft, barely noticeable, particularly with the howling wind.

Okay. She was fine. Still sleeping. And he wouldn't let her do any work tomorrow, because it had obviously been too taxing.

He was supposed to be watching out for her, not wearing her out.

He'd turned back to the bathroom to douse the light again when a gust of wind shook the cabin and the bulb crackled loudly and went black.

The fire snapped and popped, the only sound inside the cabin aside from the storm. Lightning strobed through the skylight over the round bed.

"Alex?" Nikki's voice was soft, thick with sleep. And it put him in mind of early mornings, tangled sheets and more closely tangled bodies.

"What are you doing?" she asked.

Losing his mind, evidently. "Power went out."

She sat up a little. "Really? Feels like a hundred degrees in here."

It wasn't. In fact, without the hum of the electric furnace, the cabin was cooling rapidly. A good thing on a personal front.

"What time is it?"

"Around eleven." He was glad he was standing in the shadows, pretty much out of the firelight. "You slept through dinner. I can heat it up over the fire, I suppose. Just spaghetti. Probably won't harm it any."

"I'm not hungry." She sat up a little more. "But I need to go…would you mind?"

He frowned in the darkness. "Just a second." He wasn't about to carry Nikki Day without his pants on. He wasn't into living that dangerously. His jeans were where he'd left them, lying in a heap next to the couch and he quickly pulled them on, then went back to the bedroom and scooped her off the mattress.

Heat radiated from her like the furnace would have done had it been operating. He stopped cold. Pressed his hand to her forehead. She was sweating. "You're burning up."

"Just a little too warm," she murmured. "The, um, the bath—"

"Yeah. Yeah." He carried her carefully into the bathroom and set her on the bench. "Hold on. I'll get you a candle."

"I can manage."

"I said hold on." Testy, still feeling the heat of her, he retrieved one of the candles that lined the mantel and lit it effectively by shoving the tip in the fireplace. Then he carried the fat, squat thing into the bathroom and set it on the sink. "There."

"Thanks."

He closed the door and paced back to the fireplace. Kept glancing toward the bathroom and catching his lightning-splashed reflection, along with the round, mammoth bed, in the mirror.

He wasn't going to barge in on her in the bathroom again, but waiting for her to call for him took more patience than he'd have liked. When she did so, she'd pulled off her sweater and wore only a thin, sleeveless shirt that clearly defined her swollen belly, plus the taut thrust of her full breasts.

But with more skin showing, he could feel even more fully just how hot she really was. "You're running a fever," he muttered. "I'm taking you to the hospital." He didn't pause, even though he expected an argument. But he got none.

Which made him move all the faster. He blew out the candle before going into the bedroom to set her on the bed. "What'd we do with your shoes?"

"I don't know. I haven't worn them since we got here." She curled onto her side, obviously wanting to go back to sleep.

"I knew I shouldn't have let you do any work." He finally found her boots—one under the bed, the other nearly hidden beside the nightstand.

"I'm not running a temp because I sorted some mail."

He closed his hand around her ankle and she stilled, audibly sucking in her breath.

"What's wrong?" he demanded.

"Nothing."

Didn't sound like nothing. But she didn't pull away, and he finished working her boot over her stockinged foot, then repeated the process with the other one. "I've got to bring the truck around from the shed. Don't go anywhere."

She groaned a little at his poor joke.

He went into the living area and yanked on a sweater and boots, then shoved his arms through the sleeves of his coat. The keys to the SUV were still hanging on a hook near the door where he'd left them when they'd arrived.

"Be careful," she called just as he let himself out into the howling wind. He yanked up the collar of his coat and trudged off the steps in the general direction of the shed.

With no moonlight and no flashlight to guide him—a candle would've been useless with the wind—it was slow going. But there was little between the two structures to impede his progress, and fortunately, it wasn't snowing.

Nevertheless, he managed to clock himself in the head on the log building, and swore viciously as he groped his way to the swinging door and heaved it open.

Climbing inside the SUV at last, he started the engine, flipped on the blessed headlights and drove right up to the steps of the cabin. Alex left the passenger door open and hustled inside.

Finding Nikki's coat, he pulled it over her bare arms, then picked her up and carried her to the truck.

"I'm sorry about this," she murmured as he nudged her fumbling hands out of the way, to fasten the safety belt himself.

"I'm the one who's sorry," he countered. Sorry he'd let her lift a single finger. Heat was coming off her in waves, and he hoped to hell it was because of the contrast between her and the freezing conditions outside.

Certain that she was tucked in safely, he slammed the door and strode around to the driver's side. In seconds, they were heading down the road, buffeted by the wind.

"This is terrible weather to be driving in. Nobody should be out in this." Nikki shifted in her seat, obviously uncomfortable.

He'd have driven faster if he weren't afraid of sliding off the damn road. "No better than back home." He shot her a quick look. Her face looked tense in the green glow of the dashboard lights. "If you had to have a vacation now, why not pick someplace warm at least?"

"Cody and I were going to spend our honeymoon in Lucius. That's where his parents stayed. They spent their wedding night at Tiff's."

Alex's fingers tightened on the wheel. The tires spun a little as he turned onto the highway, heading to town. Who the hell was Cody? "*Were* going to spend," he repeated. "Is *he* the father—"

"I wish." Her comment was barely audible. Then she cleared her throat. "He died before the wedding."

Alex had always known Nikki hadn't sprung from a

rock the day she'd begun working for him. But he'd never asked what sort of life she'd actually had.

"He was only twenty-two," she said after a moment. "And you were…"

"Twenty-two, also." She gave a quick sigh. "He had an undiagnosed heart condition. He died on a Thursday afternoon during football practice."

The lights of Lucius were visible now. Alex had the accelerator pressed to the floor and the SUV flew down the road. Twenty-two. They'd been babies. "Must've been tough." An understatement.

"Umm." Her head fell back against the seat. "I came to Lucius to put things to rest. Seems like all I've done is stir things up. Caused inconveniences wherever I went."

He snorted and wheeled into the hospital parking lot, shooting straight up the ramp to the emergency-room entrance. "Gonna send out invitations for the pity party?"

The comment had the desired effect. She stiffened, fortunately no longer looking on the verge of tears.

He parked dead center of the entry and went around to carry her inside. As soon as they entered, along with a blast of howling wind, a nurse hurriedly produced a wheelchair, and Alex settled Nikki on it.

"Labor?" The nurse cast a critical eye over Nikki, undoubtedly noting that she looked nowhere near term even swaddled the way she was in her thick coat.

"Fever. Backache. Dr. Carmichael was treating her less than a week ago."

"Ah. I was on vacation last week. We'll pull your

wife's record in a sec." The nurse, a comfortably middle-aged woman who radiated calm, smiled at Nikki. "But first let's get you to a room where you'll be more comfortable. Your husband can fill out the paperwork and join you when he's finished." She didn't wait for a response, but sailed backward through a swinging door, pulling Nikki's wheelchair after her.

She's not my wife. The words sounded inside Alex's head.

But as he turned to the desk, where a bleary-eyed clerk waited with pen in hand, he didn't voice them.

The question was, *why?*

Chapter Seven

"A bladder infection!" Nikki couldn't contain her relief. She'd been lying in the examining room for what seemed hours.

"It's not uncommon." The doctor on duty this time was a woman. "I was plagued with them with each of my three pregnancies, in fact." She glanced over the top of her modern, black-framed glasses. "My doctor advised me to drink more water. Of course, I was already drinking enough water to float a cruise ship, but that was beside the point."

She scribbled her pen across a prescription pad, tore off the small sheet and handed it to Nikki. "Antibiotic. Take them until they're gone. And drink more water." Her lips quirked. "If you're not feeling considerably better within twenty-four hours—and by better I mean no fever whatsoever—call us immediately."

"And she still needs to stay off her feet," Alex confirmed. He'd been leaning against the opposite wall, doing a good imitation of a stone pillar for nearly an hour, with his arms crossed over his wide chest and his expression unreadable.

"Absolutely." The doctor flipped through the chart. "Dr. Carmichael wants to see you next week, I see. Monday. He'll undoubtedly reevaluate you at that point." She smiled. "Assuming we don't see you again over the weekend." She tucked her pen in her lapel pocket. "Your temp is just about normal now, so unless you have any questions or other concerns, you can blow this pop stand." She raised her eyebrows, waiting.

Nikki shook her head, and with another admonishment to drink more water, the doctor handed over the insurance forms and left.

Nikki stared blindly at the pale pink forms. Once again, Alex had footed the bill. "I'm sorry."

"For not drinking enough water?" His voice was dry. "For scaring another couple dozen gray hairs onto my old head?" He straightened away from the wall, picked up her coat from where it was draped over a straight-back chair, and spread it across her shoulders. Then he scooped her off the exam table and settled her in the wheelchair. "At least while we were in here the storm blew itself out."

Nikki propped her head on her hand, still staring blindly at the slip the doctor had given her. "The hospital probably has an all-night pharmacy."

"Good thing. Doubt there's any other place in Lucius that's open at this hour." He pushed her out into the waiting room. "You going to be okay here while I get that taken care of?"

She nodded. He plucked the scrip from her fingertips and strode away, swiftly querying the admissions clerk about the location of the pharmacy. He was nearly to the elevator when Nikki called his name.

He stopped, turning on his heel. "Yeah?"

His hair was tousled, the gray strands he'd joked about barely visible. His jeans were stiff with mud around the hems. He needed a shave and his eyes were bloodshot.

He looked as far from her impeccably dressed, workaholic boss as he could get.

Something unraveled inside her. The something that kept a barrier between the unattainable and…everything else.

She swallowed. "Thank you."

His head tilted. Then his lips quirked in a smile before he stepped into the elevator and the doors slid closed.

Nikki exhaled, shaken. She felt as if all the vibrancy in the sleepy waiting room left with him.

She glanced around. Three other people sat in the molded chairs circling the room—an elderly woman dozing over the mound of knitting in her lap, and a young couple clinging to each other's hands, their eyes tired and glazed.

Nikki's expression was probably not much different.

She rested her head on her hand, closing her eyes, dozing just a bit. How on earth would she ever repay Alex? Not just for the money he'd spent, but for his *time?*

For a moment she actually wished she'd cashed Hunter Reed's abhorrent check. What would be worse? Using *his* money, or being in Alex's debt?

At least she respected Alex.

He could be a hard man, true. But he had integrity. To the core.

He would never evade his responsibilities. Nor would he ever substitute someone for another in a fit of weakness.

"Here."

She started, looking up. Alex held a small white bag in one hand and a bottle of water in the other, and he dropped them in her lap. She wrapped her fingers around the water bottle, bemused. This was a hard man? A man who fixed her meals, carried her hither and yon, put up with her cabin-fever moods? "You're turning into quite the nursemaid," she murmured.

"I don't want to see you go through what Valerie did when she lost *her* baby."

Had it not been for the sealed lid on the water bottle, Nikki would have pushed the contents out in a geyser when her fingers tightened spasmodically. "Valerie was pregnant?"

Dear Lord. Was *that* why Alex had been spending so much time with his ex-wife? Because they'd been having a child together?

"Pull your coat closed." The entrance door slid open as they approached it, and he wheeled her outside. "It was a long time ago. Back when we were married. Tore her up emotionally, though."

Nikki looked up at him, her emotions righting themselves. Nearly.

The SUV was still parked right where he'd left it— a testament to just how quiet the night at the hospital had been. "And you?"

"The baby was the reason we married." He pulled open the door and lifted her into the front seat.

Nikki only stared harder at his divulgence. Her perception of him had been making subtle, yet discernable shifts since she'd wakened to find him beside her hospital bed.

This shift, though, wasn't subtle at all.

"Were you in love with her?" She would never have voiced the impulsive question even two weeks ago.

"I've known Val since we were kids. Love her? Yes. *In* love with her?" He shook his head, closed the door and rounded the truck.

When he got in and turned the ignition, he glanced at Nikki. "You hungry? Think you could eat something now?"

"I…" She lifted her shoulders, unable to formulate even the simplest of answers.

"Evidently there *is* something other than the hospital that's open all night. Pharmacist told me there's a café somewhere on the main drag. Thought we could stop by and I'll grab something to go. But if you're too tired—"

"No. It's fine. Maybe we could eat there. A change of scenery would be welcome."

He looked ready to argue.

"We could check with the doctor."

He frowned a little. And proved how sick he was already of his own cooking attempts when he went back inside the hospital, returning a few minutes later.

"Okay. You're cleared for a brief field trip. But we're not going to linger." Alex drove out of the parking lot. "You've gotta be as sick of my cooking as I am."

"Not at all." Then she smiled a little as she turned her gaze out the side window. "You push microwave buttons better than I'd expected."

He was silent for a minute, then let out a bark of laughter.

The sound rippled down Nikki's spine. "If I were allowed to sit up more, I could cook," she said wistfully.

"*You* cook?"

She slid a look his way. "Ordinarily, I'm capable on a lot of fronts."

"Frighteningly so," he drawled.

"I bake, too." There was probably some self-help book that would have preached against her promoting her homemaking abilities, but something in his bland voice egged her on. "I have a killer brownie recipe. My grandmother's."

His gaze didn't waver from the road, but she had the strongest feeling he was fighting amusement.

Embarrassed, she shut her mouth and wished she hadn't begged to go to the restaurant.

It was easy to find the café, since it was the only building with light shining from its front windows. A sign proclaimed it to be Luscious Lucius. Despite the late hour, there were several other vehicles parked in the slanted parking spaces in front.

Alex turned off the engine and looked at Nikki, his wrist hung over the steering wheel. "Soon as you get an all-clear to sit up for more than five minutes every hour, KP is *all* yours," he assured her. "And you can show off your brownies all you want. Until then, you're not lifting a finger. Not even to open the courier pouch from Miriam."

Now *that* wasn't what she'd wanted at all. "But—"

He lifted his hand. "I can't take another night like tonight. I'm an old man, Nik. Have some pity."

She exhaled with disbelief. "You're not old."

His mouth twisted wryly and he shocked her speechless when he suddenly twisted out of his coat and yanked his sweater over his head, leaving him in nothing but an undershirt that hugged every sinew.

"Here." He handed her the sweater.

Her hands automatically closed over the soft wool. "What are you doing?"

"Put it on. You need it more than me."

"But I'm not cold." She'd practically shrugged out of her own coat already, thanks to the SUV's heater.

He looked pained. "Just put it on, will you?"

"But—"

"That shirt you're wearing is fine with me," he stated, "but it might shock the patrons of the Luscious Lucius, here."

She automatically looked down, then flushed. The

shirt *was* thin, and even as she began fumbling her arms out of the coat to pull his sweater over her head, she could feel her nipples tightening under Alex's gaze.

The gray cashmere garment was miles too big for her, but it was enveloping. And if her breasts tightened even more beneath *his* sweater when he climbed out of the truck and came around to retrieve her, then only she knew it.

"You're *not* old," she reiterated when he carried her inside the café, an act that garnered startled looks from the handful of occupants.

He chose a booth near the window and tossed their coats on the empty table next to it. "Honey, I'm no kid anymore."

Honey. She suppressed yet another shiver at that. But he was right. He was not a kid. He was a grown man.

All grown.

After every incident of him carrying her, she had to force her heart back down into her chest where it belonged. It should have gotten less disturbing over the days.

It hadn't.

Her thoughts were scattering again like a bag of loose marbles. She blamed it on the sweater, which smelled like him. "My helping you with the stuff Miriam sent is *not* what caused my infection." Returning to the argument in question was definitely wiser than dwelling on her emotions where Alex, personally, was concerned. It had been bad enough when he was her unattainable boss—remote and preoccupied with a million duties.

"If you hadn't overtired yourself—" He broke off, shaking his head.

She couldn't bear the expression in his eyes. He blamed himself. She stretched her hand across the table, closing it over his wrist as he reached for the laminated menus tucked between the sugar bowl and saltshaker. "I *still* would have ended up with the infection. Things like that usually take more than a few hours to come on, Alex."

His hooded gaze dropped to her hand and she swallowed, quickly releasing him. But her palm still felt his warmth, and she curled her fingers, her knuckles pressing against the cool laminate tabletop.

"Coffee?"

She nearly jumped out of her skin when the waitress spoke beside them, and she felt idiotic when Alex's eyebrows rose at her betraying start.

"Hon?" The waitress held up the glass coffeepot and Nikki swallowed down the wave of longing at the sight. Alex immediately flipped over the sturdy white mug sitting in front of him on his scallop-edged paper place mat.

"Specials are written on the board over the counter," she said, deftly filling his cup as she nodded over her shoulder at a sizable chalkboard hung above the counter, where a half-dozen stools sat empty. "Or you can order off the menus if you prefer." Her voice was pleasant.

Alex's gaze cut to the board. "Short stack of pancakes. Two eggs, over easy. Wheat toast. Bacon, crisp."

The waitress didn't bother writing any of it down. Nikki figured she was far too experienced to need notes. "And for you?"

Nikki was suddenly ravenous. "The same, please. No bacon, though. And—" she slid Alex a quick look "—water to drink. Thanks."

"You bet."

The waitress moved on, filling coffee cups as she made her way back toward the kitchen. She stopped, though, when another person entered the café. "Still have a slice of pecan pie waiting for you, Sheriff," she said in greeting.

The newcomer doffed his cowboy hat. "Sounds real fine, Jen." His gaze traveled over the occupants, as if assuring himself that all was well in his world, then he stopped next to their table. "Nice to see you up and around again, Ms. Day."

"Nikki, please."

He glanced at Alex for a moment, then back at her. "How's the Tucker place working out for you both?"

"It's, ah…" Words failed her.

"An interesting place," the tall sheriff finished, looking vaguely amused. "Believe it or not, it's better than the other rentals around here."

"How's Hadley?"

For a moment, the man's gaze hardened a little, but it was fleeting. "She's good. Taking some time off. Our sister, Evie, plans to take over running Tiff's."

"Would you tell her I said hello?"

He nodded. "You two let me know if you need anything while you're staying in town. Don't want you to have bad memories of the place once you head back home."

Nikki couldn't prevent herself from glancing at

Alex. Only she found him watching her, and looking away seemed incredibly difficult. "I won't," she finally answered.

The sheriff smiled, but it didn't last as he slid his phone out of his pocket and peered at the display. He sighed. "Duty calls." He settled his cowboy hat back on his gleaming blond head and turned to leave, calling out for Jen to hold the pie, after all, as he went.

"*Are* you going to have bad memories?" Alex lifted his coffee mug, his gaze unwavering over the rim.

Nikki finally dropped her eyes, staring hard at the place mat in front of her. Would she have regrets? "I came here to put memories away," she murmured after a moment. Memories of an impossibly sweet boy she'd loved. Memories of an impossibly demanding man whom she hadn't known as well as she'd thought.

"So, how's that working out for you?"

Alex's voice was droll and it startled her enough that she looked up. One corner of his mouth was tilted, and his gaze seemed uncommonly gentle.

And even as that fact tugged at those unraveling threads inside her, she felt the melancholy drift away, and she smiled, too.

There were parts of Alex that she'd obviously *never* known. And she was finding them impossible to withstand.

She pressed her spine against the back of the booth, rubbing her hand over the cashmere and feeling the rhythmic thump of the baby inside. "Working out like gangbusters." By some miracle her voice was nearly as dry as his, and when the baby finally stopped kicking, she felt a squeeze in her heart, caused by the crinkling of Alex's eyes when he smiled.

Then the waitress arrived, bearing their laden plates.

Nikki sat back a little, surreptitiously drawing in a long breath as Jen set out the meal, refilled Alex's coffee, brought a second glass of water for Nikki and disappeared again into the kitchen.

The silence was oddly comfortable as Alex and Nikki dived into their meals, and when she couldn't finish her pancakes, after all, Alex slid her plate in front of him and ate the rest.

Even though he'd spent days now carrying her about, the intimacy of that one act hit her hard.

She wasn't sure whether to be grateful or not when he made short work of it, then paid the check and carried her back to the truck.

The return drive to the cabin was accompanied by the lulling song of the tires on the road. And by the time they arrived at the cabin, holding up her eyelids was taking a concerted effort.

The chill was immediate when he carried her inside.

The fire had died while they were gone.

Alex stopped inside the door, leaving it open to catch the thin moonlight. "Try the light switch."

She reached out, sliding her hand over the wall until she felt the switch. But nothing happened when she flipped it. "Electricity is still out."

He kicked the door shut behind them and doused even that small bit of light. "It'll warm up as soon as I get the fire going," he said as he made his way to the bedroom, as deft as a jungle cat in the dark.

He settled her on the bed and reached around her for the bedspread, inadvertently brushing her belly. "Sorry." His voice was low.

The spread settled over her, but even with that and the coat she still wore, she shivered. "Maybe we need to call someone about the power." She peered through the darkness, trying to follow the sound of his movements.

Above her, the skylight loomed like a gaping hole.

"We'll know by morning. You'd think a place like this would have a gas furnace, instead of electric."

She heard the scrape of a match, saw the blue spark, smelled the sulfur. The match dropped into the fireplace and bit into the kindling that Alex must have stuck there.

The red glow from the fire slowly crept into the bedroom, and she could see him more clearly, hunkered down in front of the fireplace as he coaxed the flame. Because of the darkness, she couldn't see through the fireplace to the couch on the other side. It was reasonable that the heat from the fire would warm that side of the cabin just as easily as it would the bedroom.

Her fingers bunched the heavy bedspread, sinking into the soft velvet. "Maybe you should sleep on this side," she said quickly, before she lost her nerve. "You know. On the bed. It's bound to be warmer than the, uh, the couch, with just the quilt you've been using."

She saw him turn his head, look at her over his shoulder. He had yet to remove his long black coat. But she couldn't even hope to see his expression. "That's not a good idea."

She clutched the velvet tighter. "I don't know why not," she said, practicality overshadowing the uncertainty she felt. Barely. "This bed is enormous. A family of five could sleep on this thing with room to spare."

He didn't respond.

Uncertainty nosed ahead of practicality. "Unless I, um, snore or something."

He turned back to the fire, tossed another piece of wood on, sending a shower of sparks up the flue. The logs snapped and popped. The cozy scent of burning pine wafted gently her way. "You don't snore," he finally said.

"How do you know? Maybe I do. Just not loudly enough for you to hear me from the living area."

"I know."

"But—"

He uncoiled, rising in one fluid motion that had whatever she was going to say balling up in her throat. "I know," he said evenly, walking toward the bed, "because I hear every breath you take at night." He leaned over, planting his hands on the mattress on either side of her head and leaning down within inches of her. "Because I hear every sound you make, period. When you turn over and the sheets slide against you. When you fumble around on the nightstand to find your glass of water, or your book, or your cards to play another game of solitaire. I know."

Her lips parted, shock streaking through her, followed hard by something else entirely.

"And that's why it is not a good idea for me to sleep in this bed no matter how damn cold it is. Because there isn't a bed wide enough for me not to know you're there, too." He exhaled, sharp and short. "And if that isn't clear enough for you, Nikki, then maybe this is."

He caught her head in his big hand and pressed his mouth hard to hers.

She went still. Her mind went blank and for one protracted moment, it seemed as if the universe and everything in it stopped moving.

Then his thumb brushed down her cheek and his lips gentled.

Everything that had gone still slammed into whirling, spinning motion. She lifted her hand, needing something to steady herself, and found his forearm, his wrist. She could feel his pulse throbbing.

His lips nibbled, explored, tasted, and she discovered there was nothing steadying about him, after all. A foreign sound rose in her throat and she angled her head.

Nikki was vaguely aware of the soft pillow cradling her neck as his fingers tightened in her hair. Her lips parted and he delved deeper.

Devoured. She felt devoured.

And just as the hazy realization hit her that she wanted more, he tore his mouth from hers.

His lips burned along her jaw. His forehead pressed against hers. His breath came fast, hard, stirring her hair. For an instant, his hand tightened in the strands that tangled around them.

Need clamored inside her and she thought he would kiss her again.

And the fact that she wanted it, desperately, was enough to yank her to her senses.

What was she doing?

He abruptly released her, shoving himself off the bed. If she hadn't been prone, she would have swayed.

"I'm sorry." His voice was low.

"Of course." Hers was just as low. She wasn't even sure he'd hear. Naturally he was sorry. She was someone he'd depended on, and now was someone he pitied.

And she didn't even have the spine right then to summon her defenses over it.

But he did hear. "Aren't *you?*"

Sorry? She couldn't begin to answer that. How many times had she entertained the fantasy of kissing Alex?

But a fantasy was all it had ever been.

And now…now…

Oh, Lord, she could still taste him on her lips. "I don't know," she whispered.

"Well, you should be sorry," he said, his voice suddenly as businesslike as if they were standing in the middle of Huffington's conference room. "We can't take things like that back, Nikki. Can't pretend it didn't happen. Particularly when we've just spent three hours at the emergency room."

And she was well and truly exhausted, as a result. Which was probably why her eyes were burning and her throat felt like a vise had clamped around it.

She should be grateful that he was standing a good

four feet away, because it was the only thing that prevented her from reaching out, futilely, for him again. She just lay there, aroused beyond anything she'd ever experienced—from just a kiss!—and mortified because she seemed to be the only one there who didn't regret it.

Well, hadn't she always known that Alex wasn't interested in her that way? If he had been, he'd have had ample opportunity in the three years she'd worked by his side to do something about it.

"I'm sorry to have offended you," she said stiffly.

"God, Nikki. For being one of the brightest women I know, you are so totally clueless I could strangle you." The conference room voice was gone, replaced by hard irritation.

He took a few steps toward the fireplace. Wheeled around and paced back. "Dammit. You think I kiss women who offend me? I don't want to get in that bed—no matter how bloody cold it is—because I don't think I can *stop* at a kiss. And that's a helluva note, isn't it? Because I'm supposed to be here trying to watch out for you, trying to protect you, not putting the bloody moves on you while you're carrying another man's child!"

Chapter Eight

Alex heard his voice rocket around the bedroom, and wanted to strangle himself even more than he did *her*.

The fire popped behind him and he looked over to see a narrow log split into pieces, collapsing in on itself in a shower of sparks that faded as quickly as they'd flared.

He exhaled. "It's been a long day. We're both tired. So let's chalk it up to that and pretend none of this ever happened."

She didn't reply.

Given the way he'd pounced on her, then barked at her, could he blame her? Still, he found himself hesitating, and for a man who hesitated as rarely as he lost his temper, it wasn't a comfortable realization.

"I'm sorry," he said again.

She was so quiet. He hoped to hell he hadn't scared her into tears or something. He'd never been particularly moved by female tears before, but Nikki in tears undid him.

"Take your antibiotic."

"I already did. At the restaurant. While you were paying the check."

Her voice was calm. More like the Nikki he knew.

Too calm? Not calm enough?

Christ. He was losing his mind. He tried to shake off the insanity that had him in its grip. "Do you need anything else?"

"No."

"Good night, then."

"Good night."

He turned to leave.

"Alex?"

God. He needed to get out of her bedroom in a serious way. "Yes?"

"Thank you. You know. For everything you've done for me."

"Are you saying that now to remind yourself why you can't be angry with me for..." He waved his hand. For kissing her. For stopping. For doing whatever it was he'd done to make her quit her job.

He wanted to curse the conscientiousness that was such an intrinsic part of her nature.

"Yes." She made a soft sound of annoyance. Or maybe hurt.

He didn't know.

Couldn't tell.

Where the hell had his objectivity gone?

"Forget about it," he said brusquely.

"I can't." The velvet bedding rustled. He could see her sit up in the bed. "And not because of…well, just now. But because I think you're helping me because you expect me to go back to Huffington."

"I've told you that's not the case."

"Then what is the case?" Confusion rang in her voice. "It's not that I don't appreciate what you're doing for me, Alex. I do. But I don't understand what you're getting in return!"

"And I do nothing without a return on my investment."

"Alex, I…" She made another soft sound.

He sighed. "Is it so inconceivable to you that I have no ulterior motive?"

She hesitated.

"Speak up, Nik."

She exhaled. "You said that to me the second day I was on the job."

"I meant it then. I mean it now. If you have something to say, then say it."

"All right!" She sounded pushed. "Yes, it is *inconceivable* to me."

That's what came of trying to help a woman who'd handled nearly every detail of his life in or out of the office. She knew that he usually got what he wanted, one way or another. "Maybe I want an answer," he said. "One that makes sense."

"An answer to *what?*"

"Why you left me."

She went quiet.

"And don't give me that crap that you gave me in your resignation letter, about taking the position with Huffington as far as you could. That you needed a different, fresh challenge, or some such baloney. You loved that job." He couldn't have been that wrong about her.

"But it was just a job, Alex! It shouldn't have been my whole life."

"Was it?" He paced back and forth. "Was it your whole life, Nik? Obviously it must not have been, or you wouldn't have gotten pregnant somewhere in there toward the end. Is the father someone from Huffington? A staff member? A patient?"

"I've already told you he wasn't!"

"Then why the hell did you leave me?"

"Leave you? You keep saying that, Alex! I quit my job. Period."

"You were always one of the most honest people I knew. I counted on it. And you're lying now. And damned if I can figure out why you'd go to the trouble unless the answer has something to do with me or Huffington. If it's someone on my staff, do you think I'm going to let him run out on his responsibilities?"

"Don't presume to think you know me so well," she said stiffly.

"Oh, I know you." He paced. "I know you used to walk down to the corner drugstore about three times a week, even in the dead of winter, to get yourself a scoop of pistachio ice cream. I know you read decorating magazines when you ate your lunch—usually a yogurt with some weird granola crap tossed in—at your desk. I know you're allergic to grass and you got your hair trimmed every eight weeks on Tuesday mornings, while I was meeting with the department heads. Your favorite movies are old romantic comedies—black-and-white, preferably—and you're afraid of spiders but you'll catch one and move it outside rather than just step on the damn thing."

He stopped pacing. Stared at her in the firelight. "I know that no matter *what* I tossed your way at the clinic, you could handle it. You're an MBA. More than capable of running an institution on your own if you wanted to, but you were my assistant and I counted on you. Out of all the women in my life, you're the only one I ever counted on. And you walked out without one single reason that I can accept. Was I really that impossible to work with?" He knew he sounded like a blithering idiot, and the knowledge did *not* improve his mood.

"You weren't impossible to work with." Her voice was thick. Husky. "Not that Miriam would agree with that these days," she added, in an obvious attempt to lessen the tension weighing down the room like a soggy, wet blanket.

"Then why, Nik?"

"If you're trying to soften me up—"

"Would it work if I did?"

"No."

"Then what does it matter? Just tell me what I did that drove you away."

"*You* didn't do anything, Alex."

"But someone did. If not the father of your baby, then was someone else hassling you over something? You know I don't tolerate that kind of—"

"Nobody was hassling me. You did nothing wrong. Just…leave it alone, Alex. Please."

He paid no heed to the faint break in her voice. "You're just letting this yahoo walk, without taking any responsibility at all for the baby."

"It doesn't concern you!"

He inhaled. Exhaled more slowly. "Then why does it feel as if it does?"

She didn't answer.

And he knew he was right. If he weren't, she'd have said so. Instead, she didn't say squat, because she wouldn't tell him an outright lie.

But knowing it with more certainty than ever didn't make him feel any better.

And driving for the truth while she was in a fragile state was about as low a thing as a man could do.

So he left the bedroom before he made matters worse.

He grabbed the poker and jammed it into the fire a few times, stirring it up, and tossed on a log large enough to burn for most of the night. Then he grabbed the quilt and threw himself on the couch, closing his eyes.

But he didn't sleep.

After a long while, he got up again and rummaged through the stuff from the courier pack. He found the calendar he'd asked Miriam to send. It was one of the few things in the pack that he'd actually *requested*.

He sat on the fluffy rug in the firelight and flipped open the book, paging back to the previous summer.

Nikki wasn't being forthcoming about what had happened the previous summer.

He couldn't pretend any longer that he didn't want to know why. And he didn't like knowing that he strongly wished Nikki would have confided in him.

Unfortunately, the suspicion that hit him as he refreshed his memory made all too much sense of his questions.

Alex was in the shower.

Nikki lay on the bed, staring up at the soft blue sky through the skylight overhead, and listened to the hiss of the water. She assumed it must be hot enough, judging by the curls of steam seeping out beneath the closed bathroom door.

The electricity was restored, at least. It had clicked on sometime midmorning. It might have been easier on them if it had simply remained out. Then they would have had no choice but to make other arrangements. To leave this un-honeymoon cabin.

She rolled on her side and stared at the bathroom door.

A foolish endeavor, since it only encouraged her to imagine Alex standing beneath the needlelike spray.

As if her imagination needed any help.

Her fingers touched her lips. He'd clearly regretted kissing her the night—morning—before, which made her overwhelming desire for more kisses, more…*more,* all the more humiliating.

Somehow, she doubted the stress of staying here with Alex like this was what Dr. Carmichael had in mind when he'd ordered bed rest.

The water continued hissing. Alex had been in there longer than usual. Ordinarily, he was a five-minute shower kind of guy.

And when in her entire life had she ever imagined she'd know *that* particular detail about Alexander Reed?

She rolled onto her back and stretched her arms and legs. Trying to stay prone was all well and good, but she was definitely getting stiff from the inactivity.

Stiff and *not* relaxed.

She heard the familiar toot of a horn outside.

The courier had arrived. Earlier than usual.

But instead of leaving the forbidden-to-touch pouch on the step, as he had the other days, the driver knocked on the door.

"Alex!" Nikki raised her voice so he could hear. "The courier is here."

But the shower didn't stop.

And the knocking on the front door was growing impatient.

She sighed. Untangled her legs from the bedspread and went to the door herself, feeling as if every muscle in her body was screaming. Two minutes on her feet to answer the door shouldn't be a disaster. She spent more than that upright when she was getting in and out of the shower, which the doctor had assured her was fine.

But walking through the living room felt distinctly odd. She glanced at the couch, where Alex was spending his nights, and opened the door.

She blinked in the bracing rush of cold air, then had to blink again.

Not only the courier stood there in front of the cabin.

Valerie Reed stood there, as well.

And she seemed equally surprised to see Nikki in the doorway.

Her vivid green eyes widened, going straight to the swell of baby beneath Nikki's dark flannel tunic. "Well," she said after a moment. "I guess I understand what Alex is doing here *now*."

"It's not his." Nikki's face went hot as she blurted the words.

Valerie's smile looked tight. She adjusted the stylish red scarf over her shoulder. "It never is, darling." She looked past Nikki. "Is it, Alex?"

Nikki looked over her own shoulder.

Of course.

Now he comes out of the shower.

And the sight of him made her catch her breath. Hard.

His jeans were barely fastened, and the towel slung around his neck did little to stop the water from dripping down his torso, glittering against the whorl of hair sprinkled liberally across his hard chest.

"Um, ma'am? Could I get a signature here?"

Nikki felt like some cartoon character caught in a weird universe. She turned to the courier standing next to Valerie. She'd all but forgotten him.

She took the pen he offered and scribbled her name. "You haven't needed a signature before."

"Looks like a cell phone." He handed over a small box, and reached past her to set the fat pouch inside the door, but his gaze hardly left Valerie.

Why would it?

The woman was blond and stunningly beautiful, and looked like she belonged on the cover of a fashion magazine rather than the step of this cabin.

"Have to cover our tracks on delivering them," he said, "because so many get stolen." He backed off the rickety step, watching Valerie as long as he could before climbing into his truck and driving off with a spit of gravel.

"What are you doing?" Alex spoke behind her, and she turned to face him, stepping out of the way so Valerie could come in out of the cold, as well.

Nikki wasn't certain which one of them he was questioning, but judging by the displeased look on his carved face, she could make an educated guess. "I'm signing for *your* cell phone, since you didn't hear the door." She lifted the box slightly. "Excuse me," she murmured to Valerie, and set the box on the back of the couch as she passed Alex.

He smelled of soap from the shower, and was entirely too appealing.

In the comparison department between herself and Valerie, she'd never come out on top.

"Where's she going?" Valerie asked, as Nikki sank down on the bed she was coming to loathe.

"She's supposed to stay off her feet."

Nikki pulled an extra pillow over her face, trying to block out their voices. As a suffocation device it was pretty effective. Otherwise, it did little good.

She tossed the pillow away and turned on her side, covering her ears with her hands.

Alex entered the room, glancing at her. One eyebrow rose a little at the sight of her playing monkey-no-hear, but he continued into the bathroom and closed the door.

"How far along are you?"

The ground was not going to swallow her whole, no matter how much she wished it.

She lowered her hands, which were as ineffective as the pillow had been, and looked at Valerie, who was standing beside the fireplace. Not in the bedroom, but not outside it, either.

The lovely red scarf and black coat were gone. She wore a skinny black turtleneck and equally skinny black pants that made her look even more willowy and ethereal.

"Nearly seven months," Nikki answered.

"Alex said he was taking care of something here in Montana. I never dreamed it would be you." Valerie's voice wasn't unkind. Merely surprised.

And why not?

Alex's actions *were* surprising.

"It's good that you're taking the doctor's advice, though," the other woman added. "You can never be too careful."

"Alex told me about your—"

"Miscarriage?" Valerie finished as Nikki hesitated. "Yes. Well. *I* didn't follow my doctor's advice." Her eyes were sad. "I didn't follow a lot of good advice, actually." Her lips turned up at the corners. "I'd like to think I'm smarter about such things these days, though."

Feeling as if she'd entered a movie theater well after the film was in progress, Nikki could only manage a vague nod.

Then the door opened again, and Valerie looked as relieved at Alex's appearance as Nikki felt.

The towel around his neck was gone. His wet hair was no longer spiking around his head in appealingly boyish waves, but was slicked severely back from his face, and that bare, stunning chest was covered by a navy, cable-knit sweater.

Did he wonder at all what she'd done with the sweater he'd tugged over her head the previous night?

He barely gave Valerie a glance as he walked over to the bed. "You probably have clothes that need laundering."

And talking about it—emphasizing the fact that his staying with her entailed more than just being a present body—in front of his ex-wife was about the last thing Nikki wanted to do. "Is there a washing machine lurking in this cabin that I don't know about?" She managed to inject a note of humor into her voice as she awkwardly pushed a pillow behind her stiff back.

"Alex, really. As if you'd know what to do with a washing machine, anyway," Valerie said, laughing at the idea.

And even though Nikki had thought the same thing

herself, she felt annoyance twitch along her nerve end-ings. "Actually, Alex is pretty adept at appliances these days," she told Valerie. Then glanced quickly up at him. "But I can manage on the clothes issue." She'd have to start washing her lingerie in the bathroom sink, because she'd gone through the supply of clean undergarments she'd brought with her to Montana. Not that she intend-ed to discuss *those* details with Alex, whether his ex-wife was present or not.

She may have slept in his sweater, tucking it away that morning alongside Cody's old jersey, but she was *not* going to discuss the state of her underwear!

Judging from his expression, though, he'd read at least some of her thoughts plainly enough. He reached over her, causing her breath to stall, until she realized he was merely grabbing one of the bed pillows. With a quick shake, he tugged off the slippery pillowcase and tossed the bare pillow back on the bed. Then he hand-ed her the empty case.

"Put whatever you want washed in there. I'll have someone in town take care of it." He then plucked her suitcase off the chair and set it on the bed beside her. "I'm arranging for more groceries to be delivered. The fridge is about empty. Is there anything in particular you want?"

She tucked her tongue between her teeth for a mo-ment. It had to be her imagination that he was making a point of their enforced domesticity. "A reprieve from bed rest. You think they're stocking that on the shelves in Lucius?"

His lips twitched. "Probably not." His dark gaze drifted over her. "How are you feeling?"

He could pretend that his ex-wife wasn't watching them avidly, but Nikki couldn't. "Self-conscious," she murmured under her breath. "Maybe Valerie would like some coffee or something," she said more naturally.

Alex glanced over his shoulder. "Coffee's in the kitchen," he said brusquely. "Help yourself."

Nikki's eyebrows shot up, but Valerie merely shrugged and turned. A moment later her slender, black-clad legs passed the fireplace again on her way to the kitchen.

"Well?" Alex was watching her. "You're pale. What's wrong?"

"Maybe you should see to Valerie?" Nikki's voice was little more than a hissing whisper.

"She's capable of pouring herself a cup of coffee," he assured her, his tone dry. "Why are you sitting so oddly?"

"My back is stiff from all this inactivity. Don't you think you need to see why she's here?"

"I know why she's here."

Foolish, foolish Nikki. "You invited her." Of course he had. Hadn't he and Valerie been nearly inseparable in the months before Nikki had quit?

"No, I did *not* invite her." His voice was as low as hers. "Hell, I've been trying to—" He broke off, looking irritated.

Trying to *what?*

Nikki had no chance to ask because Valerie sauntered

back into view, sipping from the oversize mug that Alex often used to serve Nikki's soup at lunch.

"So…" She leaned her shoulder against the fireplace mantel. "Whose mess are you cleaning up this time, Alex?"

Chapter Nine

Alex had to curtail the urge to throttle Val as color flooded Nikki's creamy cheeks. He turned his head, focusing a warning glare on his ex-wife that she seemed to take inordinate glee in ignoring.

"Whoever it is must be important," Valerie stated blithely. "Why else would you take time away like this while the Macfield deal is still on the table?"

"Macfield? You were working on that deal last year. I thought it was supposed to be a slam dunk." Nikki's voice was only slightly strangled, due to Val's incredible lack of tact, but her surprise was still plain. Rightfully so, since she'd sat in on a good number of his early meetings with George Macfield.

And trust Valerie to bring it up.

Just then, Alex couldn't begin to remember any of the reasons why he continually tried to help Val help herself.

"It should've been," he answered.

"And it would have been," Val interjected, "if George Macfield hadn't gotten wind of a bidding war between Huffington and RHS for his little shop of horrors."

Alex raked back his hair and shot Val another look. "Macfield isn't a shop of horrors."

Val shrugged. "All of their equipment looks like it's straight out of a science fiction movie."

"*RHS* wants Macfield? But why?"

Alex looked back at Nikki, oddly grateful that she, at least, could focus on the point even when Val seemed bent on mischief. "RHS *doesn't* want Macfield." His family's health care empire had more resources than the devil himself. "But they know that *I* need Macfield."

"I'm…still not following," she murmured. "Why would your family want to prevent you from expanding?"

"Because that's the way my father works. If he can improve RHS's hold in the market while at the same time destroying the one thing I managed to accomplish without him, he'll die a happy man."

"Oh, Alex," Val scoffed. "Your father doesn't want to destroy Huffington. He wants to add it to RHS."

It's the same thing, he thought.

"But this is crazy!" Nikki sat forward so abruptly Alex figured she meant to launch herself off the round bed, and he took a hasty step forward. But she seemed to catch herself when he moved.

"I can understand why any health system would want

to add a gem like Huffington to their fold, but why the interest in Macfield?"

"To force my hand. They can't buy me out, because I refuse to sell to them. But if they make it impossible for me to continue expanding, then they know the clinics will ultimately fail, because I won't be able to keep my edge in the industry. If I don't want every single one of my employees to be standing in the unemployment line, I'd have to sell. Either to RHS or another health system."

"I still don't see what's so bad about that." Valerie's voice was reasonable. "You stand to make a fortune. Your family's offer is a good one."

"A fortune isn't what Alex wants." Nikki's voice was quiet, her gaze focused on him only until he met it. Then her slender throat worked in a quick swallow, and she looked away. "Huffington isn't about money. It's about being the best teaching and clinical center, about leading the industry in research. That's what's important to Alex. Helping people. Whether it's a seven-year-old soccer player or an eighty-year-old stroke victim."

"Honey, you don't have to trot out the company line to me," Val murmured drolly. "I'm in public relations, remember? I'm well aware of Huffington's mission."

Alex watched, oddly caught by the subtle flush that rose in Nikki's cheeks. It was easier to blame the warmth inside his chest on that than the fact that Nikki seemed to understand something about him that his ex-wife, a woman who'd been in his life all of his life, didn't.

Huffington's mission was *Alex's* mission.

But Val had never been able to recognize that the two were indistinguishable.

He shoved up the sleeves of his sweater. "Put your laundry in the pillowcase," he told Nikki, then turned to Val. "I'll meet you outside."

Val's eyebrows rose a little. But she lifted a shoulder and sauntered back into the living area to collect her coat. A moment later, the door opened and closed behind her.

Too bad the relief of her absence was only temporary. He'd wanted her to return his phone call. He hadn't wanted her to show up here.

"Is RHS a real threat, Alex?" Nikki's voice was quiet.

"It wouldn't be if the old man hadn't learned I was after Macfield. Can't blame George Macfield, though. He's just holding out for the best deal."

"Why didn't you say something about this before?"

Nikki didn't seem to be making any move to fill the pillowcase, so he opened her nightstand drawer and pulled out all the contents, pausing only momentarily as he recognized his own sweater.

"What are you doing?"

He pushed the clothing, sweater and all, into the pillowcase. "Taking care of things."

She snatched the case from him, clutching it protectively. "Because you think I can't?"

He sighed. Sat on the edge of the bed and eyed her.

Her blue eyes were dark. Vulnerable.

Had she always been so vulnerable?

Or was it just her brushes with him, his family, that had done it?

"Because I *can*."

Her brows drew together. "I don't like feeling…beholden."

"You don't like feeling as if something is out of your control," he corrected. That was going to prove even more problematic unless he did something about it.

The corners of her soft lips twitched wryly. "Well. There is that," she allowed. "I owe you, Alex. And I…well, I don't know what to do about that."

"Come back to work?" He lifted his eyebrows, his voice deliberately light.

She huffed, but the faint smile stayed in place.

It was a helluva time to realize he'd prefer to sit on the side of the round bed with Nikki and her faint smile than go out and deal with Val.

"Add the rest of your clothes," he said as he rose. "Maybe Val will prove useful and drop the stuff off in town when she leaves."

"But I thought—" Nikki broke off.

He paused, waiting. But she just waved her hand dismissively. He watched her for a moment longer.

Fresh color filled her cheeks and she made a shooing motion with her hands. "Valerie is probably freezing outside."

He supposed it was possible. But if he knew Val—and he did—she rarely let herself be uncomfortable for any length of time. Still, he turned and left the cabin, grabbing his coat along the way.

Outside, Valerie was leaning against the hood of her rental car, cozily wrapped in coat and scarf, her nose buried in the coffee mug as she watched his approach.

He stopped several feet away. "Okay, Val. What has Hunt done now?"

She tried looking innocent, but failed miserably. Same way she always had whenever it came to Alex's cousin. "You're the one who's been leaving me messages all over Cheyenne," she reminded him.

"To which the usual response would be picking up the phone and returning the call. Not traipsing all the way here to Lucius."

"Which is a seriously small town," Val said humorously. The effort to sidetrack him was ineffective.

There was only one thing that would have distracted Valerie from her increasing dependence on Alex. The one thing that had always come first—for better or worse—with Val. "Hunt?" he pressed.

Her eyes narrowed with annoyance. "Not everything in my life centers around Hunter, Alex."

He lifted an eyebrow. "You've made an effort this past year at trying otherwise. But the only thing that has ever pushed you out of your box has been Hunt. So, what'd he do?"

She stared into her coffee mug, her finger slowly tapping the rim. "He's leaving Elizabeth."

Alex barely paused at that. "This is news?"

Val flinched a little and he sighed. "He's been saying he's going to leave her since about two weeks after he married her." Alex waited a beat. "Twenty years ago."

"Eighteen," Val corrected stiffly.

No matter how irritated Alex got with her, he still had a soft spot for Valerie. Protecting her was as natural to him as breathing. But the on-and-off relationship she'd maintained with his cousin for her entire adult life was beyond his comprehension. It always had been.

He scrubbed his hand down his face. Beneath his boots, the snow creaked. He looked at the cabin, picturing the woman inside. In Nikki's position, Val would have run screaming to him to save her reputation and her ego.

Nikki Day, however, stood straight and walked alone.

He eyed Val. She was taller than Nikki and her reed-thin figure possessed none of the curves. Her hair was as blond as it had been when she was five years old, and her eyes were green. Today, they weren't bloodshot, which he considered a small blessing, and maybe some indication that she was finally finding some peace in her life. Maybe.

It wouldn't stay that way, though, if she didn't see Hunt for what he was.

Alex felt as if he were walking yet another tightrope, and this one was thinner than the Huffington-Macfield-RHS deal.

"Are you here to tell me you're quitting and going back to the family fold in Philadelphia?"

Her expression tightened. "I don't live for *my* career, darling," she reminded him.

He let the familiar dig pass. "Did you finish the prep for the Valentine's Day dance?"

"Not quite." But she waved her coffee mug as soon as the words left her mouth. "Don't look at me like that. We're doing local radio spots next week. Not just in Cheyenne, but also in Phoenix. It'll all be fine."

"And then?"

She lifted one shoulder, looking sleek and languid. But he knew it was an act she'd cultivated long ago. "Then Hunter says he's going to meet me in Arizona. We're going to take some time off together."

The nightmare worsened. "How much time?"

"A few weeks. Maybe more."

"He needs to be at RHS's next board meeting."

"You don't worry about me coming back to work, but you *do* worry about Hunter being at the family's quarterly board meeting. You're *so* good for my ego, darling."

"I worry about a lot of things where Hunt is concerned," Alex said grimly. "He's never been faithful to Elizabeth *or* to you. What makes you think any of that has changed?" *He* knew his cousin hadn't, and wished there was a way of convincing Val of it without everything blowing up in his face.

"Hunter has never missed a board meeting," she said, a little too doggedly.

"It's about the only thing he hasn't missed." Hunter was reliable about a few things: womanizing, stringing Val along and keeping himself in the monetary favor of the almighty Reeds. "Don't get involved with him again, Val." He eyed her when she didn't respond. "I see. You already are."

"Please don't be angry with me, darling. I can't take it when you're mad."

How any woman could be so wise to the world on so many fronts, yet remain so blind to one man, was a mystery to him. "Things won't work out the way you hope, Val. I don't want to be picking up the pieces again when they don't."

"There won't be any pieces," she insisted.

"There are always pieces."

"Not this time." Her smile was brilliant and brittle enough that if he hadn't already been worried about her, he would have started. She stepped forward and hugged him tightly. "Please don't be miffed. You know I hate it so."

He patted her back and sighed. That was Val. She'd never understood that he wasn't mad. Only saddened by someone wasting her hopes on someone completely unworthy.

"Alex?"

Val turned her head beneath his chin as they both looked back at the doorway.

Nikki stood there, one hand clutching the door, the other rubbing her swollen belly.

He stepped around Val and strode toward the cabin. "What's wrong? Why are you out of bed?"

Her gaze avoided his as she extended an arm. He realized she was holding her cell phone. "It's Miriam. She's pretty desperate to talk to you."

He took the small phone, his fingers brushing hers, and she quickly turned back inside, closing the door. He eyed the solid wood panel for a long moment, then put the phone to his ear. "Yes?"

Miriam's voice was high-pitched with anxiety. "Your father's been calling you all day. He's looking for you."

Great. "Did you tell him where I was?" He could practically hear her gulp.

"Yes," she squeaked.

He wanted to snap at her for being so gullible, but something prevented him. The memory of Nikki chastising him because Miriam had always been afraid of him.

Hell. He didn't want people afraid of him.

That was his father's tactic, not his.

His jaw ached, though. "It's fine, Miriam," he told her after a moment. "Let me know if you hear from him again."

She sounded tearfully relieved as she assured him she would, and ended the call.

"Problems?"

He pushed the phone in his pocket and eyed Val. "You'd better drive back to Billings while it's still light. You've always hated driving after dark. And make sure Hunt gets to that board meeting."

She eyed him oddly, then nodded and handed over the coffee mug before climbing into the car.

He didn't wait to watch her drive away.

He went back inside, carrying the mug into the kitchen.

When it rained it poured.

"Alex?"

He flipped on the faucet and rinsed the mug, then left it in the sink. "I'd better not come in there and find you standing up again, Nik."

She didn't respond and when he went into the bedroom, she was lying in the center of that round bed. She looked concerned. "Where is Valerie?"

"She left."

Her brows knit together in a motion that was so quick he thought he might have imagined it.

"Are you all right?" she asked.

"Any reason why I wouldn't be?"

"I wish…" She hesitated, her gaze flicking up to his, then away again. "I wish you'd told me about RHS and Macfield."

"Why does it matter to you?"

She winced. "I care about what happens to you—your company. What are you going to do?"

"Hope to hell that Hunter votes against RHS's acquisition of Macfield at the quarterly meeting. He's the only one who might conceivably go against my old man's wish to put me out of business, and it'll take someone with that large a share of stocks to vote it down."

Her face tightened a little and he felt the impact in his gut.

"Your cousin?" Her voice was careful. Too careful.

And he knew. If there had been any question that his suspicions were off base, her schooled, painfully cautious expression eradicated it.

"Hunter." Alex kept a tight rein on himself. "You've met him."

"Yes." Her voice was thin.

"Who knows what game he's playing, though." He went on deliberately. "Hunt has always been a law unto himself. Figure he's the one who spilled the beans about my interest in Macfield in the first place."

Her fingers were busily pleating the edge of her loose flannel shirt. "W-why would he do that?"

"Probably because he was pissed that Val left Philly and came to Cheyenne."

She swallowed. "Why would your cousin care that you and your ex-wife were getting back together?"

"Back together? Who said anything about that?"

"She was in your arms!"

"Val's a hugger. So what?"

"Well—" She broke off. Began again. "You gave her a job and—"

"Because she needed one."

"You two were always together—"

"Because we've known each other since we were kids."

"So I thought you were…reconciling."

"Not in this lifetime. She's in love with Hunt," Alex finally said, watching Nikki closely. "Always has been. And he—as much as he's capable of, anyway—is in love with her."

"But…"

Alex waited.

Nikki shook her head a little. Pushed herself up against the headboard, her movements stiff. "She was *your* wife," she finally finished.

"I was a substitute for Hunter," he said flatly.

Her eyes widened. Her face went scarlet, then white.

When she pressed a sudden hand to her belly, he cursed himself. "Are you okay?"

She moistened her lips, not meeting his eyes. "Fine," she whispered.

The anger seeped out of him, leaving him feeling older than his years. What was Hunt's hold on the women in his life?

And when had Alex begun thinking Nikki Day was a *woman in his life?*

The pillowcase full of her laundry was lying on the floor next to the bed. He picked it up. "I'll get this taken care of," he said. "And find a masseuse to come out for you."

"Excuse me?"

"A massage. That's about the only thing I can think of to alleviate a stiff back, since you're not climbing in a bathtub anytime soon."

She looked bewildered. "But…but that's just extravagant!"

"So?"

She pressed her palms to her face for a moment. "You have to stop spending your time and money on me, Alex. It's going to take me forever and a day to pay you back."

He realized he was staring at her abdomen, and looked away. "I wasn't aware that we'd drawn up loan documents."

She dropped her hands. "I can't keep accepting your generosity, Alex. It's not right."

There was no way he would get into a discussion with her on what was right and wrong. "We've done this song and dance a few times already. It was out-of-date the first time."

"I don't want a masseuse," she said, sounding close to tears.

"Then I guess you'll have to make do with me," he said after a moment.

The words were true on more levels than one.

Chapter Ten

"All right. Where does it hurt?"

Nikki drew up her knees as far as they'd go, wrapping her arms securely around them. "Honestly, Alex. There's no need."

"I told you I'd help work out your kinks."

She swallowed, her glance flitting around the bedroom's unsubtle interior.

"Maybe I should rephrase that."

"Quite possibly," she agreed, not certain whether she was more embarrassed or amused.

"It's me or a massage therapist. Make up your mind."

Alex was sitting on the side of the bed. She'd already managed to put him off for most of the evening. But dinner was a memory now, and his mind was obviously set.

Just as his mind was apparently set against reconciling with his ex-wife.

Another major shift in what she'd believed about him.

A substitute for Hunter?

Surely it would have been the other way around. Hunter wasn't even a good substitute for Alex, as far as Nikki was concerned. There wasn't one admirable trait she could think of in relation to Hunter. Yet Alex was filled with them. How could Valerie not have preferred Alex?

"Really. I'm fine." Nikki stretched out her legs. Pointed and flexed her toes. "See? I've healed myself." And he didn't need to prove the point that he wasn't likely to be overcome with lust by putting his hands on her.

The kiss they'd shared was nothing to him but a momentary blip in judgment. It had not been a heartfelt craving for her. That was her problem where he was concerned, and hers alone.

"Healed." He snorted and solved the matter simply, by closing his hand over her ankle.

By some miracle, she managed not to climb right out of her skin. He drew her foot onto his lap, his fingers kneading her arch through her thick white sock. Despite herself, she couldn't prevent a groan.

His lips quirked. He kneaded a little harder and her head fell back against the pillow.

So much for willpower.

She willingly offered up her other foot.

"Guess my technique isn't so objectionable, after all," he said wryly.

"It's not polite to gloat."

"Yeah. But you know the worst about me. So what's the point of politeness?"

She looked at him from beneath her eyelashes and sternly warned her clamoring hormones to back off. "The worst? And what exactly is *that?*"

He shrugged. "Take your pick. Demanding. Self-centered. Arrogant. Workaholic who puts the job at hand before everything and everyone."

She considered that. "Well, you are demanding," she allowed. But he didn't demand more of anyone else than he demanded of himself, and generally less. "And you *can* be arrogant." She supposed, given his background and all that he'd accomplished, he'd probably earned some of it.

The corner of his lip tilted and a dimple creased his lean cheek. "Gee, Nik. Thanks."

Heat winged through her bloodstream when his thumb explored her anklebone.

"It's more like you're completely confident in yourself," she stated, keeping her voice level with an effort. He was looking down at her feet, and she sucked in her lower lip, struggling for control. "As for being self-centered, or always putting work first, I'd think your presence here proves the fallacy of that. You're not getting *anything* out of this, Alex. And I'm painfully aware of that fact."

"I don't know." His fingers massaged the back of her heel and he shot her an inscrutable look. "Maybe I have a thing for feet."

She stared. But then his dimple deepened and she realized he was teasing her. She made a face and rolled her eyes and hoped it hid the fact that she was trembling inside.

"It's actually not bad here," he said after a moment. "Being away from the office hasn't made me go stark raving crazy yet."

"It's not exactly been a vacation for you."

"As close as I've been in a while." She could hear the smile in his voice. "Maybe I owe you."

"Please," she murmured dryly and he chuckled softly.

His kneading fingers worked their way up her calves, and she alternately cursed and blessed the fact that she was wearing jeans, because they were too narrow around her ankles to allow any contact with her skin.

Despite the denim, he was more than adept at finding all manner of tight muscles, though. "You're pretty good at this," she finally acknowledged.

"I *do* run a sports medicine clinic."

"You run several." She watched him awhile longer. He planted her foot flat on the mattress, his hand behind her calf, working up toward her knee. Nikki wanted to know what had happened to Valerie and the baby. She wanted to tell him she was sorry that his ex-wife had loved someone else. She wanted…so many things that were increasingly impossible.

"What *do* you plan to do about RHS?" she finally asked. "You're not really going to just depend on your cousin's support, are you?" The notion was completely out of character for the Alex she knew.

Thought she knew.

"Depend on Hunter?" His lips twisted and his expression darkened so much she wished she hadn't brought up the matter.

But then he looked at her and his face smoothed again. His fingers began kneading once more. "I haven't depended on him since we were eighteen. Instead of striking out with me like we'd planned, that's when he dutifully fell right in line with the family plans for him. What college. What studies. What wife. He bought into every last bit of it."

"You sound like you were close once." Despite Hunter's occasional visits to Huffington, she hadn't been under the impression that remained the case. Because of Valerie?

"Why the sudden curiosity?"

Nikki avoided his eyes. "No reason."

He found a knot in her calf and tarried there, working on it. "People didn't just think we were twins because of the resemblance between us," he said after a while. "They thought we were twins because we were the same age and thick as thieves." He slanted a look at her. "You're the one with a real twin, except you and Belle hardly resemble each other at all."

She didn't want to dwell on the physical resemblance between him and his cousin. That's what had led her into trouble. "Belle got our father's dark hair and eyes. I got our mother's blue eyes and red hair."

"Auburn."

"On a good hair day." She would *not* put her hand to her hair the way she self-consciously wanted to do.

She'd braided it that afternoon, but the waves never really wanted to stay contained, and lying around the way she was didn't help matters any. She was also two inches taller than her sister, and even when Nikki wasn't pregnant, she'd generally cursed the curves she'd been saddled with, while her sister, the fitness maniac, was as svelte as a racehorse.

"Val's dad was as entrenched in RHS as somebody not born a Reed could be. It was a foregone conclusion that she would marry into the family one day."

And so she had. "You had already started up Huffington when you two married, though, hadn't you?" Which was a little odd, given that Alex had *left* the RHS empire by then.

He nodded, but didn't seem particularly inclined to elaborate on that point. "My father raised me to be an independent thinker," he finally explained. "And then couldn't understand why I wanted my own shop outside of the family. He cut me off when I didn't toe the line, and I headed west. Hunt was supposed to come with me. But he didn't."

"And you ultimately founded Huffington in Cheyenne," she murmured. The PR material on how Huffington began was clear in her mind. She was certain the details didn't come close to the grueling reality of what Alex had accomplished, almost entirely on his own.

"That's where I was stuck when my funds ran out. Where I met Earl Huffington."

"He was the administrator of the old hospital, right?"

"Yeah. He staked me to get my first clinic up and running." Alex's hand paused, resting on top of her knee, his gaze turned to the past. "Died the same year I finally operated in the black."

"That's a shame."

He nodded. "Earl was a character. How he managed to keep the old hospital afloat was nothing short of a miracle. The guy was as much a rancher as he was an administrator."

"Did you know him before you arrived in Wyoming?"

He shook his head. "I was broke. Needed a job. Went to the only place where I had experience—hospital administration." He shifted off the mattress. "And the rest is old news. Turn over and I'll do your back." When she hesitated, he frowned. "*Can* you lie on your stomach?"

"I know I look like an elephant, but I'm not that big yet." She rolled over, tucking a pillow beneath her to help even herself out.

"You don't look like an elephant," he assured her dryly. "Can't even tell you're pregnant looking at you from the back. What does that mean when a woman carries a kid all in front like that? That she's having a girl or a boy?"

Nikki folded her arms beneath her face, bracing herself for the moment his hands touched her again. "Boy, supposedly."

"Do you know for sure?"

"You know I've had ultrasounds. Not just here in Lucius, but back in Cheyenne. But, no. I don't want to know for sure." The mattress dipped as Alex sat back down and reached over her. Her mouth parted and she hauled in a silent breath when his fingers curled over her shoulders, his thumbs working in deep circles along her spine.

"Going to find out the old-fashioned way," he murmured. "That's about what I'd expect from you."

"Is that supposed to be a compliment, or not? Oh. Lordy. Right there." He'd found the point midway down her back where it felt as if she had iron bands instead of muscle.

"Just a statement of fact," he murmured. "Tell me if I'm pressing too hard."

It was heavenly. "Don't let it get out at Huffington that you've got hands like this, Alex. You'll end up working in physical therapy if you're not careful."

"I'll leave PT to the experts, like your sister."

Nikki turned her face to one side, trying not to groan with pleasure, and could see their reflections in the mirror across from the bed. His head was turned away from the mirror, though, focused on her. She couldn't see his expression. Could only watch the angle of his wide shoulders, the way his lean torso was turned at the hips toward her.

Her mouth was dry. She lifted up a little, enough to reach for the glass of water that was forever ready on the nightstand. She swallowed down most of it before setting the glass back, relieved that he'd figure she was following doctor's orders rather than trying to quench a thirst for him that was not *ever* going to be satisfied.

She was well aware that he still hadn't said what he intended to do about RHS.

"Does your father really understand what it'll mean

to Huffington if RHS nabs Macfield out from beneath your nose?"

"Of course."

"But you're his son."

"So? My father would be the first to say that family has no place in business. Ironic, considering he believes business is family. And he made it more than clear twenty years ago that if I'm not with him, I'm against him. He promised to live long enough to see my downfall."

"No."

"Miriam's call this afternoon was to warn me he's trying to track me down."

Even more horrified, Nikki looked back until she could see him, not just his reflection. "Would he come *here?*" Her voice was little more than a squeak, and she winced inwardly.

"I doubt it. He's never come to Wyoming. Can't see him coming to Montana, either. He's got no reason at the moment to do so. I talked to George Macfield after Miriam gave me the heads-up, and even if RHS's board approves the acquisition, George is still on the fence."

She propped her chin on her hand. "I just can't imagine a family like you've described."

"Don't try," he advised. "It's too twisted. Might damage the baby before she even gets here."

Nikki smiled a little, as he'd meant her to. But it didn't last. "I'm sorry about your and Valerie's baby."

His hands seemed to hesitate, but maybe it was only her imagination. "She took it pretty hard. She was almost six months along."

Nikki could feel sympathy for Valerie, just as she would for any woman who lost a baby. But her heart didn't ache for the other woman. It ached for Alex. Who thought he was only a substitute for a man who wasn't worth a fraction of Alex. "It must have been hard for you, too."

"Yeah."

She pushed up on her elbows, looking at him over her shoulder. He seemed surprised by his stark admission.

"Maybe it was better, though," he said after a moment, shaking his head. "In the end. Given the way we were all raised, maybe it was a reprieve for an innocent child not to be raised by any of us."

"Oh, Alex. That's not…"

"True?" He gently nudged her back down, by flattening his palm against her spine. "We value business success over relationships. God forbid I'd have ended up being the kind of father I had."

"You wouldn't have raised your child the way you were raised, because you *do* have a different value system than your father," she murmured, her face against her folded arms once more.

"You sound pretty sure about that." His voice was suddenly husky.

"Of course I'm sure," she said without hesitation. "You're a good man, Alex. You'd make a good father."

The silence following her statement went on just a little too long for comfort.

"What about your mother?" she asked quietly. "You haven't mentioned her in all this."

"My mother is the ultimate society matron. Very well coiffed and well heeled to anyone outside the Reed fold. Ever since I can remember, she's had an affair every summer with the new gardener."

Shock rippled through Nikki. "How do you know that?"

"Everyone in the family knows. My parents' estate sees a new crop of gardeners every single year. Always a litter of young, buff guys from which she can choose. But as soon as Labor Day is over, she's back in propriety's graces again. She'd no more screw the gardener after Labor Day than she would wear white." His tone was exceedingly dry. "And there's an ugly peek into the world I inhabit."

Nikki pushed herself up on her elbows again. His hands paused at her waist. "*Used* to inhabit," she corrected. "You were what—eighteen?—when you left. You're forty-two now. You've been out of that world longer than you were in it."

"A person's past can seem like a guest come to visit in the present, sometimes."

"A guest who's outstayed her welcome." Nikki knew all about the hold a person's past could have on the present. "That's pretty much the reason I came to Lucius. Because I was finally determined to put my past with Cody into the past and keep it there."

She'd realized she *had* to do something when she'd found herself marking off another anniversary of his death and feeling as if the wound was never going to heal. That had also been the day she'd realized Valerie had been back in Alex's life for more than six months. Not that she'd needed any reminders, but on that day, the anniversary of Cody's death, Valerie had gone breezing past Nikki's desk into Alex's office, gaily telling him they needed to celebrate their six-month anniversary.

And she'd heard him laugh, and agree that a celebration was indeed in order.

Nikki had lost Cody long ago. She'd *never* have any sort of chance with Alex.

She'd called Tiff's that very afternoon and made a reservation. She'd also gone out with some co-workers after work for happy hour at the Echelon, surprising them a lot more than she had herself. And when she'd run into Hunter Reed there, she'd stopped fending off the flirtations he always had at the ready whenever he came to Cheyenne to visit his cousin.

She'd been tired of being alone, of hurting, and she'd only ended up making her life more complicated.

"I stayed at Tiff's because that's where Cody and I had planned to spend our honeymoon, same as his parents had. I tried to go on a sleigh ride because he'd promised we'd go on one each day we spent here. The man who drove the sleigh? I think his name was Ivan." Some details of the day she'd collapsed were still fuzzy in her mind. "It wouldn't surprise me if he was the man who'd driven Cody's parents around back then. I had it in my head that if I just spent some time at Tiff's, if I went on that sleigh ride, then I'd finally stop—"

"Grieving?" Alex's hands weren't kneading now. They were simply holding.

She had a nearly overwhelming urge to turn around and rest her head on his wide chest. To let him hold her and let everything—all the stress of her pregnancy, her work situation, her memories of Cody, her confusion over *him*—just fall away.

She curled her fingertips into the pillow under her elbows. "Wanting things I couldn't have," she said quietly.

"But you didn't get your sleigh ride, did you?"

She shook her head, amazed to find her lips tilting in a rueful smile. "Not exactly. I got the hospital…and you."

"Some days you're the windshield, and some days you're the bug."

She tucked her tongue between her teeth for a moment. "I think that's a line from a song."

"Mmm-hmm."

"So…are you the bug or am I?"

"Think maybe we both are." He slid his hand up her back and cupped the nape of her neck for a moment that seemed to linger. Then he let go and stood up. "Muscles feeling better?"

Every muscle but her heart. She nodded and rolled onto her back again. "Thanks. That really was above the call of duty, Alex."

He didn't deny it. "Maybe after your appointment on Monday, Dr. Carmichael will spring you far enough that you can sit in the whirlpool tub for a few minutes."

The whirlpool tub that was shaped like a heart and big enough for two. "Maybe."

"It's getting late. Think you can sleep?"

She was practically boneless from Alex's ministrations. But she was no longer sleepy. And she'd already read every magazine that was lurking in the cabin. Alex had done a thorough search for her on that point. "Not yet. I'll just watch television awhile, I guess. I'll be fine."

"You hungry? Thirsty?"

She shook her head.

He nodded. Pushed his hands in his pockets for a moment, only to pull them back out again and pick up her water glass. He disappeared for a moment and returned it full, with several ice cubes floating in it.

"Good thing we were nearly out of food when the power went off," he said as he set the glass on the nightstand. "Or what was in the fridge might have gone bad before it kicked on again."

"Are there any apples left?"

"One. Thought you weren't hungry."

"Well…" He already knew what a glutton she could be. What was one more instance of it? "I could eat an apple. Is there peanut butter left?"

"Barely." The dimple in his cheek deepened. "Apple and peanut butter? Together?"

"Almost as good as pistachio ice cream."

"I'll take your word for it," he said dryly, but left the bedroom again.

Minutes later, he returned with a plate, a lone green apple, and the small, nearly empty jar of peanut butter. She couldn't hide her smile at the sight of the plate. "You probably have picnics on china, too," she murmured as she plumped a few pillows behind her and sat back against the leather headboard. "Set it all here." She patted the mattress.

He did so.

She picked up the apple and the small cutting knife and deftly quartered and cored the fruit, then quartered it again. Then she dipped the tip of the knife in the jar and spread peanut butter over the juicy slice. "Try it." She held it out for him.

He eyed it, looking skeptical.

She made a face. Waved the narrow slice of apple. "Come on. Forget about caviar and toast points. Live dangerously."

"I hate caviar." His fingers met hers as he took the slice. "And there's probably something dangerous about accepting a slice of apple from a beautiful woman."

Even though she knew his amused comment was nothing more than words, pleasure still dipped and swayed through her.

Beautiful. It was unwise to take that word so seriously. She knew it. Yet she reacted to it, anyway.

He popped the apple slice into his mouth. Chewed. Swallowed. Licked a smear of peanut butter from his thumb.

She nearly choked on the bite of apple she'd taken herself.

"Hmm." His melted-chocolate gaze slid to the plate, where she'd placed the remaining slices. "How much peanut butter is left in that jar?"

She grinned.

He pushed her legs over and sat down again beside

her, rescuing the plate before it tipped sideways. "Any other treats like this you've been keeping secret from me, Nikki Day?"

Her grin faltered only a moment. The secret she kept from him was in no way a treat. "Oh, there are *lots* of things a person can put peanut butter on," she said blithely.

His gaze slanted over her. He took another apple slice after she'd dressed it with peanut butter. "Aren't you just full of surprises."

"Lots of *food*," she corrected, feeling her cheeks flush.

His smile widened, and soon she was chuckling, too.

And even when the apple was long gone, the peanut butter jar completely cleaned out, Alex safely on his side of the fireplace and Nikki safely on hers, she was still smiling.

Chapter Eleven

"Oh, happy daaay. Oh, happy day." Nikki sang under her breath as she sat on the high bar stool in the cabin's small kitchen. Alex was outside. She could hear the distinctive thwack of the ax. But she didn't worry that he was out there chopping wood again as a substitute for chopping off someone's head. She was in too good a mood.

Dr. Carmichael had been cautiously optimistic at her appointment that afternoon. No signs of infection. The ultrasound of the baby looked very good. He still wasn't particularly satisfied with her blood pressure, but he had given her permission to be on her feet for ten minutes at a time, and to sit up for twice that.

She glanced at the oven timer. She was five minutes into her twenty, and as promised, she was on KP duty.

Happily.

She had a chicken-and-rice concoction in the oven that would be ready to eat in an hour, she'd rapidly chopped up vegetables for a chunky salad that was waiting in the refrigerator, and for the finish, she was whipping up a quick batch of brownies.

At the moment, life was really good. So good, in fact, that she'd actually had a sense of fondness for the cabin when they'd returned after her exam—Nikki on her own two feet for once.

She heard the front door open, then Alex stomping his boots on the step before coming inside. From her vantage point in the kitchen, she watched him, her hands paused over the mixing bowl.

He was wearing jeans again and she would be hard-pressed to decide which look of his she preferred. Expensively tailored and dangerous looking, or casually clad…and dangerous looking.

He crouched down beside the fireplace, stacking the armload of wood he'd brought in, then briskly stoked the fire that burned day in and day out. When he was satisfied, he planted his hands on his thighs and straightened. Shrugged out of his coat and tossed it haphazardly over one end of the sectional couch, where it slithered off the leather to the floor.

He walked toward the kitchen, seeming to look at the empty whirlpool tub as he passed it.

She wondered what he was thinking. She knew what *she* thought about the tub. She'd had a painfully

vivid dream about it. And him. Lots of warm, seduc-
tively bubbling water, lots of skin, lots of…contact.

Fortunately, she'd safely refocused her attention on
the melted chocolate that she was pouring into the fluffy
mixture of sugar and butter by the time he edged into
the kitchen. The space was more than roomy enough for
one person, but it was definitely cozy with two.

Cozy. Like the tub had been in her dream.

She swallowed and tightened her hand on the small
saucepan she'd used to melt several chocolate squares.

"Smells good in here." He looked over her shoulder
at the mixing bowl. "What's that?"

She tried to swat his hand away from the glossy rib-
bon of chocolate streaming into the bowl. "Don't taste
that," she warned. "It's really—"

He'd already stuck his finger in his mouth, though.
"Bitter." He made a face.

She laughed. "That'll teach you to stick your fingers
where they don't belong." She scraped the chocolate pan
and deftly folded the mixture in the bowl. Then she slipped
her own finger along the edge, gathering some batter on
her fingertip. "Now *this* is the good stuff." She started to
put her finger in her mouth, but Alex wrapped his hand
around her wrist and licked the batter off it himself.

The large wooden spoon plopped from her hand into the bowl. Her fingers, including the one he'd just
popped in and out of his mouth, curled against her palm.

He was nodding, still holding her wrist. "*Much* better."
He jiggled her hand. "Come on. Open up. I want more."

What devil was possessing him?

She figured it was safer not to find out.

With her free hand, she fished the spoon out of the batter and held it up for him. Batter dripped down the handle, over her fingers. "Knock yourself out."

He let go of her wrist and she quickly turned away, slipping off the stool to shove her hands under the faucet and wash away the sticky batter. When she figured her expression was schooled again, she turned off the water, dried her hands on a paper towel and turned back to the stool.

The spoon was pretty much licked clean. And he had a small smear of chocolate right next to the corner of his mouth.

She tucked her tongue between her teeth and looked away, reaching for the eggs.

"So what's next?"

His arm brushed against her as he stretched across her to lob the spoon into the sink.

So much for trying to keep her composure. "Eggs." She cracked one on the side of the bowl—too hard, and had to fish out pieces of shell from the batter as a result. She dropped the shells in the trash and added two more eggs, this time more carefully.

Alex didn't budge. He continued standing there watching, his hands braced flat against the mottled granite countertop, making his shoulders bulge against the thin black crewneck sweater he wore. She stirred in the eggs, feeling completely self-conscious, until finally she looked at him, exasperated. "Don't you have something else to do?"

"One would think."

Yet he didn't move.

She lifted her eyebrows. "Well?"

"I've never really watched anyone cook before."

She made a disbelieving sound.

"I'm serious," he insisted.

"Don't you ever watch a cooking show on television? No. Scratch that. The only thing you ever watch is news. Or sports." For a "suit," he was definitely into sports. Made sense that he'd established one of the premier sports medicine clinics in the U.S. Though—she slid a glance his way again—he didn't look so much like a "suit" lately, at all. "Did you ever want to be in anything other than the health care industry?"

"Like plumbing?" His lips tilted. "There are days."

She smiled faintly. "Nuts?"

"More often lately," he replied blandly.

She picked up a small bag of chopped nuts, glad she'd had the presence of mind to beef up Alex's grocery order, which was delivered every few days. "Yes or no?"

"Yes."

Good. She loved chocolate, but put a nut in it—any kind of nut—and she was a goner. She tore open the bag and dumped the entire contents into the bowl. It was twice the amount the recipe called for, but she didn't care. The more the merrier. "Didn't you ever watch your mom cook when you were growing up?"

"My mother couldn't boil water if she had to."

"So who cooked in your family?"

Now he really looked amused. "The cook."

"How silly of me." Nikki started to reach for the pan

she'd already greased, and felt a sharp kick in her midriff. She froze. Slowly sat back, rubbing the spot on her abdomen. "Wow. Major kick. Can you hand me that pan?" She pointed.

He reached around her and pulled it close. "Does she do that a lot?"

"Kick?" Nikki nodded. "And I thought you'd decided it was a boy. Because of the way I'm carrying him all up front."

"Wives' tales," he murmured. He watched her pour the batter into the pan and slip it into the oven.

"Want to lick the bowl?" She was thoroughly amused at this boyish side of him. Amused and delighted.

"Do you?"

"Of course. What's the point of baking if you can't lick the bowl?"

"Well, if you ask me, you could have left *more* in the bowl than you did, instead of scraping it all out like that into the pan."

She handed him a clean spoon. "Eat too much batter and you'd make yourself sick."

"Who told you that?" His head bumped hers as they both attacked the bowl.

"My mother. She's the one who taught me to cook. And bake."

"Yeah, well, mothers are probably *supposed* to warn their daughters against all sorts of dangerous behavior." He tucked the spoon upside down in his mouth, clearly savoring the bit of batter clinging to it.

Nikki exhaled a little and patted her stomach. "I'm

sure she never expected to have to warn me about this. I'm the one who was supposed to have my act together."

He shot her a look. "And you *don't?*"

She was startled. He thought that? "Everybody always thinks I do." She wrinkled her nose and shook her head. "It's always *been* an act."

"Since when?" His tone was clearly skeptical.

"I guess since my father died. Belle was having a lot of surgeries—she was injured in a car accident about a year before my dad died…oh, well, you probably remember that from her working at Huffington."

He nodded. Reached past her yet again, his arm brushing against hers, to toss this spoon into the sink, as well. It clattered with a comfortable, cozy jangle.

Her thoughts scrambled for a minute and she grabbed at them somewhat desperately. "Anyway, she—Belle— was going through a lot, and my mom was having to keep things together after my dad died. I just…it was better for me not to add to the burden." Keeping herself together, putting one step in front of another, dealing with school and home, making things easier for her mom and sister wherever she could, had gotten her through that time.

"I've met your mother," he commented. "When she and…Squire?" He waited for her confirming nod. "When they visited you a few summers ago. She didn't strike me as a woman who'd consider anything to do with her daughter a *burden*."

"I know." Alex was right, of course. Nikki set aside her own spoon. The bowl was clean as a whistle. "But it was my method."

"And it's never changed. That why you found it so hard to impose upon them for help now?"

"Twisted, isn't it?"

His long fingers toyed with the handle of the old-fashioned pouring bowl. He was leaning on his arms now, his head on her level. And his gaze was steady on her. "Family dynamics. Always an adventure. Some more pleasant than others."

His had definitely been less pleasant than hers.

The knowledge of it made her hurt inside for the boy he'd been.

"Well, I adore my family, which probably makes my mind-set a little hard to understand."

"You adore them and don't want to worry or concern them, so you go out of your way to be the pinnacle of self-sufficiency. Taking care of them, in your way. Not so hard to understand."

And, it turned out, he was a caretaker, too. She would never have guessed it if not for these past several days. "You've been away from Huffington for two weeks."

"As of tomorrow," he agreed.

She focused on the smear of chocolate still near his lips. For some reason, it came home to her how he'd stuck by her for all that time. And he seemed intent on sticking until she was well enough to go home.

A tickle burned behind her eyes. She reached up and gently brushed her thumb over the smear, rubbing it away. "Chocolate," she whispered.

His lashes lowered a little. His voice lowered even more. "Is it gone?"

It was. She shook her head, blatantly lying and not caring one whit.

He started to lift his hand to rub the spot. But she caught his wrist, the same way he'd caught hers when he'd licked the batter from her fingertip. She leaned forward and pressed her mouth softly to the place where the chocolate had been.

He tasted better than any chocolate ever would.

And she'd lost her mind.

Her pulse thundered. His fingers moved and she vaguely realized her breasts were pressing against his captured arm. She slowly drew back, one aching inch at a time. "I'm sorry." Sanity ebbed back. "I shouldn't have done that."

His jaw flexed. His lashes lifted and that coffee-and-chocolate gaze captured hers.

Her mouth went dry. "And I shouldn't do this," he said, his voice oddly husky. His arm moved, and his hand covered her belly. It rested there for a moment, then slid up and gently brushed her breast.

She shuddered, his name ripping out of her in a gasp.

"You want me to stop, Nik?" His thumb drifted, smoothing over the center, which rose—mortifyingly eager—into an agonizingly pleased peak. "Say so, and I'll stop, I promise you. But I won't unless I know you want me to."

She drew in a shaking breath, which served only to push her breast against his hand even more. "I thought you didn't want—" her eyes closed when he rubbed… dragged…lingered, over her nipple again "—me." She finished on a barely audible breath.

"You're not that naive," he muttered. "I've *wanted* you for days. Since before I kissed you."

Her eyes snapped open. Her lips parted. He moved closer and his shoulders seemed to eclipse her. "You said you regretted that."

He bared his teeth for a moment and his touch became a little more fierce, before deliberately gentling. "I lied," he murmured. His palm edged upward, and she could no more prevent herself from thrusting her greedy breast against it than she could stop breathing. But his hand continued after the most tantalizing of pauses, flattened against her breastbone and moved slowly, inexorably onward until his thumb pressed against the pulse beating frantically beneath her jaw.

For some reason, the act seemed more intimate than him cupping her breast, and she trembled.

He directed her jaw until she was looking straight in his face.

"I've been blind," he said evenly. "You were under my nose all that while. A young woman with shadows in her lake-blue eyes, who put everything she had into being a better assistant than I've ever had in my life."

"I don't know what to say." Her voice cracked a little. She could feel her pulse throbbing against his thumb. It was so hard, so darn hard to be coherent, particularly when he took a step closer, turning the bar stool just enough that the V of her legs hugged him. "I thought you and Valerie—"

"No. Don't say anything," he murmured, his mouth hovering a hairsbreadth above her forehead, her temple, her cheek. So close, but not touching. He pushed her chin up a little more. "I don't want to hurt you. The baby. But if I don't kiss you in the next thirty seconds, I'm going to go out of my mind."

She slipped her shaking hands up the fine weave of his sweater. Felt the heat radiating from him as she reached his neck. Let her fingers sift through the black-and-silver strands. "Twenty-nine," she whispered. "Twenty-eight. Twenty-seven. Twenty—"

"Six." He closed his mouth over hers. Nothing tentative. Nothing exploratory. This was a complete and total annihilation of her senses.

Her head fell back. His hands threaded through her hair, tangling in it, binding her to him.

She curled her arm around his neck even as he stepped in more closely. And she groaned, starbursts pricking inside her head when he tore his mouth away to haul in a hissing breath. His hands unwound from her hair and roved down her back, captured her hips, tilting her against him.

A torrent of desire swept through her. She was shaking with it, and she rocked forward, fitting her mouth to his again just as deliberately as he'd fitted himself in the notch of her thighs.

His low growl filled her. Thrilled her. She wanted to crawl inside his skin, his very being. He caught her head in his hand, breaking the kiss, pressing her face into the crook of his neck. He laughed a little. Swore a little.

She breathed his name, exhilarated, boneless.

"You're lethal." His low voice rumbled over her nerve endings. "You have no idea."

She twined her leg around his hip, not caring if he thought she was shameless, just wanting, needing, to deepen the contact. "I'm six months pregnant," she said breathlessly. "And if you think you're going to stop now, I *will* find rat poison for your salad dressing."

His hand tightened on her hip. "We can't make love. Not in your condition."

She ought to have been shocked, but she wasn't. And she wanted to cry with frustration over the fact that he was right. She felt as if she were a thirteen-hour clock wound fifteen hours too tight. And she desperately wished that there weren't so many layers of denim separating them. She worked her hand up the back of his sweater and he jerked when she tucked her fingers against his spine a mere inch beneath the waist of his jeans.

"Nikki—"

"Shh." She looked up at him, a sigh shuddering out of her when his hand mirrored her action. "Oh, Alex."

He slid his palm upward, following the length of her spine until he nudged the strap of her bra.

She held him tighter, her head falling forward again to the curve of his neck. She was paralyzed with a deep, gnawing ache.

His hand traced the band of her bra beneath her arm, then slid over the full-to-bursting cup, drifting down into the valley between.

"You have the most beautiful breasts," he murmured.

His second hand joined the first, delving beneath royal-blue knit to explore the snug hank of satin and lace.

"You've never seen them," she protested faintly. Not only was her bra too snug, but her skin felt too tight.

"Are you kidding? I saw them plenty through that shirt of yours the night we went to the hospital. The image is burned in my head." His words burned softly against her ear. Then his fingers left her breasts and he was urging the sweater up and off, over her head.

She sat back, her hips still anchored against his, and could have wept for the way his face tightened as he looked at what his handiwork revealed. She couldn't even curse the increased fullness of her breasts or the fact that the zipper of her jeans was a good two inches from being completely fastened because of her swollen belly. Not when his feral gaze told her just how much he appreciated the view.

Her sweater seemed to fall, almost in slow motion, from his hand. "Beautiful," he repeated roughly. Then his head lowered and his mouth found the upper swell of one breast while his hand covered the other, his fingers dipping beneath the edge of the cup, sweeping within the tight space over her turgid nipple.

She trembled wildly, clasping his head to her. "Alex—"

"So responsive," he murmured, dragging the lace down until that needy nipple sprang free. He caught it gently between thumb and forefinger. His lips searched out its mate.

She was drowning. She arched against him, mindless. Never in her entire life had she been so aroused.

His fingers left her breast long enough to reach behind her, and with a deft flick, her bra loosened, fell. He pulled the straps down to her elbows, pulled the cups away from their burden, trapping her even as he revealed, and he closed his mouth over her again, with no lace or satin to bar him.

She cried out, her fingers clenching his hair, his head. His hard hips slowly rocked against her as he toyed with her nipples, tasted, teased. And just when she felt ready to scream, he dragged his mouth up the column of her throat. His lips nipped at her chin, then he covered her mouth again, his tongue sliding deep, and she convulsed in a shuddering, seemingly endless wave of pleasure.

His arms were strong, wonderful bonds holding her steady as she dissolved, boneless, finally collapsing against the back of the wrought-iron stool.

Stunned silence reigned for a long moment.

"I thought it was a myth," she finally mumbled breathlessly.

His lips were pressed gently against the pulse beating in her neck. "What's that?"

"Hearing bells." She couldn't manage to open her eyes. Every muscle in her body had vacated the building. Gone on a vacation. Probably island-hopping down in the Caribbean with the honeymooners.

She felt the faint rumble of a chuckle work through him. "That's not bells, Nik. That's the buzzer on the oven."

She peeled open one eye to find him watching her, a thoroughly indulgent expression on his face. "Oh," she said, without making any attempt whatsoever to attend to the matter. "So it is." Then she pulled his head to hers and kissed him slowly. "Truth is, though, that buzzing sound isn't the chiming I heard."

His smile was slow, lazy and utterly sexy. His hand covered her breast and there they stayed, locked together, for a long while.

Until the smell of chocolate on the verge of burning finally spurred them into motion.

She unwound her legs from him and slid unsteadily off the bar stool. Her bra fell off completely and she caught it, leaving it on the seat. Using a dish towel as an oven mitt, she pulled the brownies from the oven and set them aside to cool.

When she turned, Alex was holding her sweater. His gaze was focused on her breasts, which tightened all over again.

He was fully clothed, but his arousal was just as apparent, and her gaze did some lingering of its own.

"Don't look at me like that." He stepped forward. Pulled the sweater over her head. "Put your arms in."

She did so, and his knuckles grazed her flesh as he tugged the sweater over her breasts and down to her hips, where the loose hem covered the fact that she was too big to fasten her jeans.

"Now go lie down," he told her, slipping his palm along her cheek for a moment. "I'll finish up in here."

A caretaker, she thought again as she forced her shaking legs to carry her to the bed.

She knew that she could quit her job, run away, but there was no way she was ever going to get over loving Alex Reed.

Not anymore.

Chapter Twelve

For a moment, Nikki was blinded by the brilliant glare of sunlight off the sea of smooth, white snow. But when she blinked, she saw it.

The sleigh.

It was as beautiful as she remembered.

The ornate blue sleigh pulled by two beautifully matched horses stood behind the cabin, looking straight out of a fairy tale. She knew the red padded seat that was built for two was as velvety as the bedspread in the cabin. And the blanket folded over the seat had gleaming red tassels that she remembered, too.

Her only attempt at having her sleigh ride may have been brief, but those details, at least, were perfectly memorable.

"Alex," Nikki breathed. "I can't believe it. What have you done?" They'd barely finished their egg salad sandwich lunch when he'd told her to close her eyes, and had pulled her outside the cabin.

Now, he stood close behind her, his hands on her waist. And she really, really liked the feel of him there. The warmth radiating from him, the strength of his arms around her.

As if he'd be there to catch her if she fell.

Inside her, the baby moved in a slow roll, seeming to concur.

"So, it's a good surprise, then."

She looked up at him. "Of course. Why wouldn't it be?" She never would have expected such a gesture from Alex.

But then, everything concerning him was unexpected these days, from his presence in Montana at all, to their close encounter four days earlier over brownie batter.

Since then, they'd both kept their hands to themselves.

They were existing in an odd bubble of companionship and, well, *friendship,* she supposed, even though she'd caught him looking at her at times in the same way she knew she looked at him. And peace of mind was not equating at all to…peace.

"I wasn't sure how you'd react," he admitted, looking past her to the sleigh. "I'm not Cody."

No. He wasn't. Cody had been easy. Sweet. Loving. Not a thought in his head or heart could have been hidden on his face. She'd been a girl who'd loved him. She was not a girl any longer. And Alex was *not* easy. He was difficult. And slyly sweet. Heart-wrenchingly sexy. Dangerously unreadable. Yet even though she knew it, she couldn't make herself back away from it. From him.

"I'm amazed," she finally said. More than amazed. She was incredibly touched. "When did you arrange it?"

He helped her up onto the seat and spread the blanket over her knees. "When the sheriff stopped by here yesterday to see how things were going. He put me in touch with Ivan."

She looked around. There was no sight of the elderly gentleman who'd driven the sleigh on her first try. Not yet three weeks ago, though it felt like a lifetime. "Where *is* Ivan?"

Alex had moved over to the Morgans and was checking the riggings, as if he knew exactly what he was doing. "He'll pick up the sleigh later today."

She eyed him. "Alex?"

Evidently satisfied, he patted one of the horses' withers. "Yeah?"

"If Ivan's not here, who is going to drive this thing?"

His teeth flashed and he swung easily up into the sleigh, bypassing the short, slanted driver's seat to sit beside her on the padded one. The long reins were held easily in his gloved hand. "You're hard on my ego, Nik. Always questioning my ability."

Disbelief escaped her in a snort. "I don't doubt any of your abilities," she assured him.

He slanted her a look that was ripe with amusement and something else. Something too heated to dwell on. *"Any?"*

The fluttering inside her had nothing to do with the

baby and everything to do with him. She moistened her lips. "*Why* did you do this, Alex?"

The amusement faded, leaving only that depthless furnace. "You said you came on this trip for certain things. The sleigh ride was one of them."

He adjusted the reins a little, settling his boots on the rail beneath the driver's seat, and clucked to the horses. They bobbed their heads, and the riggings jingled musically as the sleigh gave a slight jerk and began sliding forward, heading toward the line of trees in the distance. "I figured I could play Ivan for a few hours."

Alex was no more a congenial, somewhat subservient old man than he was Cody, who'd been so easygoing it had taken Nikki's prodding to get him to finish his college work. "I used to think I knew you so well," she murmured. "But this—" she shook her head "—is the sweetest thing anyone's ever done for me."

He looked at her. The horses were walking smoothly, the sleigh moving easily through the deep, pristine snow, away from the cabin.

He brushed his knuckles down her cheek, and his leather glove felt warm. "Don't let it get out," he said after a moment. "It would ruin my image." He put his hand back on the reins.

She tucked her tongue between her teeth, battling back the utter yearning for him that was never far beneath the surface. "You don't give a flip what your image is," she finally managed to say. "You live life just the way you want to."

"And you don't?"

She shook her head. "You know I don't."

"I know you make choices and stick to them with the tenacity of a mama bear. Don't look so surprised at that, Nik. I have yet to see somebody order you around. Not when it comes down to the wire."

"You've done plenty of ordering me around these past few weeks."

"Have I?"

Had he? Or had he just stated opinions and arguments, and she'd generally seen the validity of them?

Feeling more confused than ever, she stared out over the landscape.

The horses pranced beautifully through the snow, moving just fast enough to create a slight breeze, and causing her to be grateful for the thick throw over her legs, clad in his borrowed jeans.

He'd offered several pairs to her the day after he'd seen up close and personal just how snug her own jeans had become. His were miles too long, but large enough that she could at least fasten them at the waist. Along with the throw, she wore her ivory wool coat, and beneath that, a flannel shirt layered over a thin turtleneck.

She gave in to her desire to look at Alex, beside her. She had layers to protect her from the brisk January air. He, however, wore jeans, a button-down white shirt and his coat and gloves. And the coat wasn't even fastened.

"Aren't you cold?"

He shook his head. "You?"

"I'm fine." She was chilly, but she knew if she said a single word to that effect, he'd turn the sleigh around and head right back to the cabin. And she didn't want the outing to end. Not yet.

He did jiggle the reins again. And as finely tuned as any two beings could be, the horses shifted direction slightly, pulling the sleigh in a wide, sweeping arc that brought them parallel to the glittering stream.

"Amazing the water isn't frozen over." Her breath was visible in the crisp air.

"Looks like it has a pretty swift current for such a narrow stream."

She fell silent again. In fact, the whole world seemed silent, as if taking a breather from all the details of life itself. And because it was so entrancing, that glimpse of peace where she was just a woman and he the man who was more deeply in her heart than ever, she made herself break the silence.

"How are things coming with George Macfield?"

Alex's hands tightened for a moment on the reins at Nikki's soft question. He deliberately loosened his grip. No point in punishing the horses for the tension that particular topic inspired. "They're not."

Nikki's gloved hand touched his arm briefly, then drew away.

Just as well. His control where she was concerned was worn down to a nub. He was still kicking himself for taking advantage of her the way he had when she'd been baking those brownies. Had spent sleepless hours every night expecting her to have some sort of additional crisis with her pregnancy because he hadn't been able to keep his hands off her. Because he'd been self-ish enough to drive her into climaxing for him for his own sheer enjoyment.

He'd finally resorted to calling the hospital and asking the doctor what consequences he may have caused.

Carmichael had only laughed a little and assured Alex that no harm had probably been done, though he'd warned against taking things further for a while yet.

Just thinking about "further" made Alex hard all over again. They hadn't even fully made love, and he'd never had a more satisfying moment than when Nikki had shattered in his arms.

He shifted. Planted his boots a little more widely on the rail and clucked to the horses again. They picked up the pace infinitesimally.

"Macfield told me he's going to take my father's offer," he said after a moment. "As soon as it's officially tendered, that is, which can't be done until RHS's board votes on it at the quarterly meeting in March."

That sticking point was the only thing that had kept Alex's father from already succeeding.

Nikki was eyeing him with horror, and he didn't know whether to be gratified that she seemed to have believed he could still pull the deal out of the fire, or feel even worse. Huffington was a major employer in Cheyenne, and the ripples of RHS's maneuverings were bound to be felt, because there was no way that Alex Sr. would understand Alex's loyalty in keeping the company headquartered in that town.

"And…and what about your cousin's vote? Have you spoken with him?"

"Yes," he said flatly. He didn't particularly want to talk about Hunter. "He'll go whichever way best feathers his nest."

Her finely drawn brows knit together over her elegantly shaped nose. "Oh, Alex. I can't believe this." She shook her head, then slapped her palm against her lap. "I wish there was some way for you to beat them at their own game. Take away *their* maneuvering power and see how they like it. They deserve nothing better!"

For some reason, her ire improved his own mood. "Should've figured some way to set *you* on them," he drawled wryly.

Her lips twisted. Sympathy clouded her gaze.

He looked out over the horses and adjusted his feet again.

"You need to be back in Cheyenne," she said after a moment. "Being here with me can only have made things worse for you."

Being here with her made him want to stay here with her. Quite a realization considering he'd never wanted to stay anywhere away from business. "Macfield Technologies is based in Washington State," he said. "My being in Cheyenne wouldn't have changed a thing."

"But you could have *gone* to Washington. You could have met with George Macfield face-to-face. You could have convinced him that his interests would be better served by hanging with Huffington. Macfield would end up being a household name before you were finished."

"Your confidence in me is heartening, but George's interests are more simple than that. He doesn't care what legacy he leaves in the field, he cares what financial legacy he leaves for his family. Can't blame the guy for that."

She huffed. "Well, maybe not," she allowed. "But I can blame RHS."

He smiled wryly. "It's business, Nik." God knew nothing stood in the path of his father and business.

The horses slowed as they encountered another small rise.

"Belle and Cage's honeymoon is nearly over," Nikki said after another short silence. As if she were afraid of letting the peaceful moments last too long. "I can call her to come stay with me. Or I can call one of my sisters-in-law. Someone is bound to be available."

"Tired of my company?"

"No!"

He slanted a glance her way. She looked like a princess in ivory wool, with her auburn hair drifting unfettered in the breeze. Perfectly feminine and perfectly beautiful. It was a sight that would be forever etched in his brain.

She propped the soles of her short boots on the rung next to his. The motion of the sleigh had her thigh bumping against his. "I still don't understand what you're doing here, Alex. Not when things are so critical for Huffington. But I'm glad you're here, all the same." Her admission was husky.

He pulled back on the reins and the horses obediently halted. He kicked the brake lever into place and looped the reins over the bend in it. "Why'd you quit on me, Nik?"

Her gloved fingers slowly curled. Her lashes lifted. Her eyes were bluer than any sky he'd ever seen.

She sucked in her lower lip for a moment, leaving it with a sheen that dragged at him deep inside.

"I couldn't stay," she whispered, "and see you together with Valerie. It was one thing when you were just dating a different woman every other week. But she came to Cheyenne and stayed. And you only saw her. I thought you were reconciling, and it hurt too much to hang around."

He yanked off his gloves. "Now that you know that's not the case?"

"I still can't come back to work for you," she whispered.

"I'm not asking you to." He tossed the gloves onto the floor of the sleigh. Then he turned and lifted her, blanket and all, onto his lap.

She let out a squeak, her eyes turning from sky blue to sapphire. He slid his hands along her jaw, tilting her face up to his. She was trembling. Her gloved hands slowly lifted, catching his forearms.

"But I do want you to come back with me." His thumb grazed the corner of her soft mouth and her lips parted a little. He felt the air she sucked in.

"What?" she breathed.

His thumb pressed again and her lips parted more. He grazed the edge of a pearly tooth. Her eyes grew heavy and her tongue flicked briefly against his small invasion.

"Come back and *be* with me."

"Why?"

"So many questions," he murmured. He leaned over and pressed his mouth against hers. Felt that quick intake of breath she always drew whenever he kissed her.

The need to plunder, to conquer, to seal, was fierce inside him. He'd wanted women before. But this, *this* was something else.

And it shook him.

"I want to make love to you," he muttered against her lips.

Her hands slid around his neck. She pressed herself against him as tightly as the accumulation of coats and lap robe allowed. "Me, too."

"We can't."

"I know."

"Not yet."

"I know." Her mouth opened wider under his. Her hands were strong and insistent against his head. "Kiss me." She didn't wait. Her tongue danced against his.

She was a witch. A temptress.

He caught her face again and kissed her until they were both gasping for air.

She scrambled around, slipping onto her knees, then in his lap again, even as her hands fumbled with the buttons of her coat. "Put your hands on me, Alex, before I go insane."

"It's freezing out here."

"Then why do I feel like I'm burning from the inside

out?" She dragged her coat open. "You want me to beg?" She yanked at the buttons on her shirt. "Does your ego really need that?"

His ego had taken a backseat to the desperate urgency congesting his veins. She pulled aside her brick-red flannel shirt to reveal her thin turtleneck, which clung to every generous, womanly curve. There was no question that she wasn't wearing a bra beneath the white top. The shadows of her nipples were clearly visible, their shape tauntingly beaded, and as he looked, they seemed to tighten even more.

He was aeons away from being immune, and when she, staring up into his face, pressed her gloved hands over those peaks, hiding them from view for a moment, his body clenched.

"Please," she whispered, then slid her hands beneath the fullness, seeming to offer herself up to him.

He was gone.

He ran his hands beneath her coat, catching her shoulders, hauling her up to him, taking a nipple in his mouth, turtleneck and all.

Her head fell back, her hair streaming behind her. "Alex."

He suckled until her shirt grew wet, nibbled until he could have swallowed her whole. He barely even realized she'd pulled off her own gloves and shoved his coat aside, too, until he felt the kiss of winter air on his chest, closely followed by the warmth of her slender palms. Then her fingers were flexing against him, exploring, racing downward, fumbling with his belt.

He swore. Laughed a little. "Danger zone." He grabbed her hands away and caught her mouth with his.

"I don't care." He felt her words against his lips. Felt her fingers slide between his, curling over, bringing their palms flush even as she rocked against him.

"I care." He disentangled his hands from hers, clamping them over her maddening hips. "Stop it."

She froze. Looked at him, her eyes vulnerable, panicked.

He swore again and slid his hands behind her spine, hugging her to him. "I like it too much," he assured her gruffly. "I want you too much." He proved it by thrusting himself against the notch of her thighs. "And I'm too damn old to pretend that necking in this sleigh is going to be anywhere near enough."

Her hands were caught between them, pressed flat against his chest. She flexed her fingers and he felt the soft scrape of her fingernails. "Stop calling yourself old. You're…amazing."

She was the amazing one. His rebel hands had tunneled beneath her turtleneck and crept up her spine, feeling every ridge, every inch of smooth, sweeping skin. He touched her the way he'd wanted to when he'd massaged her back.

"I want to be inside you when you climax again." He felt the ripple that worked through her at his blunt statement. "I want to be inside you when *I* do," he finished raggedly.

She moaned a little and buried her forehead in the crook of his neck. "I think it might be too late for me."

Her voice was broken, breathy, her breath warm, the flick of her tongue white-hot.

His control shattered. He pulled on her shoulders and their torsos parted, her back arching, supported by his arms, his hands. "Lift your shirt," he growled.

Beneath her lashes, her eyes glowed. She slowly drew up the hem of that clinging turtleneck. Revealed the burgeoning swell of the child inside her that couldn't be hidden by his jeans. Then the jutting swell of her breasts.

"Stop there." The ascent of the shirt stopped just high enough to reveal her peach-tinted crests.

He swallowed hard. Even through their jeans he could feel the heat of her, the incredible giving softness where he wanted to bury himself until the world went away. "We're not making love," he growled.

She rocked against him, her lips parted. Her hands flew out suddenly and she reached upward, behind her, finding purchase on the slanted driver's seat. "Yes, we are," she gasped. Her back arched again.

God, she was a beautiful thing. He surged hard against her. "I don't want to hurt the baby."

She slowly shook her head, her hair a stream of fire, her body a pagan offering to the winter sky. "Carmichael said—oh, Al…ex." It didn't seem possible for two bodies to be so close without becoming one. "He said as long as we didn't—"

He let go of her shoulders to wrap his arms around her waist, pressing her hips even harder to his own. "You talked to him, too."

Her "yes" was barely coherent.

And it didn't matter anymore what he'd thought he'd wanted before. He needed her. Now.

However much she could give. And when he slid his hand between them, cupping her intimately, she gave, and gave, crying out his name in an agony of pleasure that was too much for him to deny. When she was finally spent, he pulled her boneless form up, and she draped herself over him.

He managed to tug the tangled lap robe around her back, though their body heat was more than enough to keep them warm.

One of the horses stomped in the snow and shook his head, and the rigging jingled softly.

"Oh, Alex," Nikki whispered against his shoulder, her palm resting against his jaw.

"Next time," he repeated, in a promise. "We do it my way."

Her hand slowly smoothed over his cheek.

Whether that was agreement or not, he couldn't tell.

Chapter Thirteen

The electronic tones of Beethoven's "Für Elise" startled Nikki right out of her nap.

She sat bolt upright in the bed, blinking blearily.

Whether from the fresh air of the sleigh ride earlier that day or the headiness of Alex's lovemaking—or both—she'd been sound asleep.

The music continued and her brain clicked sluggishly into gear. Her cell phone was ringing. It hadn't rung since Alex's replacement phone had arrived, so it was no wonder it sounded foreign.

She leaned over and turned on the lamp by the bed as she picked up the phone from the nightstand. "Hello?"

Static answered her.

She frowned a little, glancing quickly at the display,

but the number shown on the readout was unfamiliar. She listened again. "Hello?"

"Nik?"

"Belle?" Nikki pressed the phone more tightly to her ear. "I can hardly hear you. Is everything all right?"

"Are you kidding me? You're the one who isn't where she belongs. You were supposed to be home from Lucius by now. Where are you?"

"I'm okay. We're still in Montana."

Static sounded. *"We?"*

"Alex is with me," Nikki admitted.

"Alex as in Alex *Reed?*"

No amount of static could disguise the shocked surprise in her sister's voice. Nikki untangled herself from the bedspread and slid off the bed, hitching up the legs of her borrowed jeans. "Yes. Alex Reed."

She peeked around the fireplace. He was not in the living room or the kitchen. She sat down on the couch and the red leather creaked. The quilt he used at night was folded haphazardly at the opposite end, and she curtailed the impulse to grab it and hold it close to her.

Would he sleep on the couch that night?

After what they'd done together in the sleigh?

After he'd told her he wanted her to come back to Cheyenne *with* him?

The fact that she hadn't answered that question ticked away inside her. How could she have answered, though?

Nothing had really changed.

She was still pregnant with his cousin's child.

She forced cheerfulness into her voice. "So, how's da island, mon?"

Belle didn't laugh and Nikki could just picture her sister glaring at the phone.

"Nikki, what is going on? What are you still doing in Montana? I talked to Emily this morning and she said you'd left some message with them that you were staying in Lucius for a while. I thought you'd have started your new job at the salvage place by now."

"Nothing's going on. I just…thought I'd stay in Montana awhile longer."

"What on earth *for?* Honey, I know this trip to Montana was sort of a pilgrimage to Cody's memory, but it's time you stopped mooning over him. We all loved him, but you've got to get back to the land of the living!" Nikki held the phone away from her ear, and still could hear her sister's emphatic voice.

She nearly jumped out of her skin when Alex appeared beside the couch and nimbly pulled the phone out of her hand, holding it to his own ear. "Belle, this is Alex."

"Give me the phone back," Nikki whispered.

He put his hand on her shoulder and held her in place. "Nikki's had a little trouble with the pregnancy, and *that's* why she's still in Lucius. She didn't want anyone worrying about her. But she and the baby are both fine. I'm making sure of it."

She covered her face with her hand. God only knew what her sister would make of *that.* Nikki couldn't hear the words, but she could certainly hear the tone of the spate that followed his statement.

"I'm here because I'm the one who was called when she was in the hospital."

"Give me the phone." Nikki held out her hand, sending him what she hoped was a stern look.

Obviously not stern enough, for he easily ignored her.

"How'd they have *my* number? Because it's the number Nikki gave when she made her lodging reservation. And I have every right to be here," he answered, to whatever Belle was saying. "Nikki's going to be my wife."

The angry buzz through the phone abruptly ceased.

Nikki blinked. Her lips parted, but nothing came out. She could only stare at Alex.

Maybe she was still lying unconscious in the pretty blue sleigh and had dreamed all this, from waking up in the hospital to the present moment.

"She'll be able to travel in another week and we'll all get together then," Alex said. "For now, she shouldn't be upset."

Upset?

She didn't think her jaw could drop any more than it already had, but she feared it might well hit the mirrored coffee table at that.

She finally sidled along the couch, away from the hand he'd clamped on her shoulder, and stared up at him. "Give…me…the…*phone.*"

"Yes," Alex said into the cell phone, evidently not intimidated by her imperiously outstretched hand. "Thank you. We're very happy. And you're the first we've told about it." He listened for a moment. "I'll tell her. Enjoy the rest of your honeymoon." He folded the phone, sliding it into his pocket. "She said to tell you she loves you."

Nikki was shaking. "*What* has gotten into you? Do you *know* what you've done? She's going to think... think that—" She was so shocked she couldn't even speak.

"Think that I'm the baby's father?"

"Yes!"

"Which means that you haven't told even your twin sister the truth."

"That's my choice." Her voice was hoarse. "My business."

"Is it?"

She frowned. "Don't go changing the subject, Alex Reed. You told my sister that I was going to be your wife! She's not going to keep that to herself. She's going to burn the phone lines telling all the *rest* of my family your little news! What on *earth* possessed you? How am I going to explain it when we clearly are *not* getting married!"

"Don't explain anything. Just marry me."

She was grateful she was still sitting. "You cannot be serious."

He sat down on the coffee table in front of her and grabbed her flailing hands. "I've never been more serious in my life. I told you I wanted you to come back to Wyoming with me."

"You didn't say *anything* about wanting me to marry you if I did!"

He shrugged, unperturbed. "So? I want you to be my wife."

Was this to be her punishment, then? For one night when her weakness had sent her into the wrong man's bed? To hear the words that she'd dreamed of, when there was no possible way she could accept?

She shook her head. "No. You can't. You don't understand."

If there was one thing she should have known about Alexander Reed, it was that the man had the persistence of ten. And the patience of twenty, when it suited him. "I understand plenty. Admit it, Nik. We're…incredible together."

"Because we have—" she steeled herself "—good sex?" They hadn't even been able to complete that particular act.

If they had, she probably would have died from pleasure.

The thought taunted her.

"I generally have good sex with women," he allowed, his lips tightening a little. "That's not all that happens between us, and you know it. It makes so much sense. I can't believe I didn't see it sooner. Why the hell it hit me so hard when you left. Why it felt like everything started unraveling."

"Because I wasn't sitting at my desk outside your office?"

"Because you weren't in my life," he corrected steadily. "I'm asking you to marry me here, Nik, not come back to work for me."

One was as impossible as the other. "I can't."

He still wouldn't release her hands. "Yes, you can. All you have to do is say yes."

"It's not that simple!"

"Yes. It is. Look. I know I'm a lot older than you are. But—"

"I don't care about your age." Her throat ached. If she said yes, she'd spend the rest of her life living a lie. And she couldn't do that to either one of them. "And it isn't simple. Just accept the fact that I cannot marry you!" Her voice broke. She finally yanked her hands free and started to slide off the couch.

But he didn't move out of her way. He merely looked at her for a long moment, the muscle in his jaw flexing, the expression in his dark eyes unreadable. "Because Hunter is the father of your baby?"

She blinked, trying to bring the world back in focus as fresh shock sucked greedily at her. "What?"

"Is he?"

She felt nauseated. How could she have been naïve enough to believe Hunter wouldn't have tipped off Alex? "*That's* why you came to Lucius? My God. I'm such an idiot. Of course you—"

"I didn't even *know* you were pregnant before I came to Lucius. But I'm right. Aren't I. He's the baby's father. He was in Cheyenne at the right time. As soon as I saw the calendar, I remembered. You were in the bar at the Echelon with a few of the women from the clinic. They go for happy hour most every Friday, but you never joined them. That evening, you did. It was the same day Hunt came to the office. He left after arguing with Val. Because for once in her life, she was actually sticking to her guns about not returning to Philadelphia and he was pissed. So he went to the bar. Met you. And a month later you quit. It's no coincidence. Hunt's—"

"Nothing," she interrupted, her voice raw. "My baby has no father. Hunter contributed some genes, and that is *all* he did."

"Do you love him?"

She gaped. "What? No!"

"Then I don't see why you're letting *him* prevent you from being my wife."

She raked back her hair. "But you don't love me. Do you?" She realized she was actually waiting—*waiting!*—for him to say the words.

And that was the biggest fantasy of all.

"Of course you don't." Her mind ticked along as furiously as her heart clenched. She finally managed to scramble past him and rise, only to regret it because her legs were shaking. "This isn't about me at all, is it? This is about the baby. Just like Valerie said. This is a *mess* for you to clean up."

"This isn't about the baby!"

Something inside her snapped. "Everything's been about the baby." She wasn't going to cry. She was not. "And if it wasn't about the baby, it was about my job! It was never about me, Alex. Not once. And I...I was stupid enough to think you...we—"

"It's always been about you." His voice rose. "Why the hell do you think I wanted you back so badly? Because I couldn't find someone I trusted enough to take a meeting for me? I have two thousand employees across the United States, Nikki. Of all people, you should know that if I really wanted to replace you, I could have!"

Tears burned her eyes. "And if I *weren't* pregnant? Would you have come to this…conclusion if I weren't pregnant?" She waited, shaking, knowing that he'd have no answer to fill the silence. "Of course not." Her words were barely audible.

He stood across from her, separated by the width of the mirrored coffee table, his hands on his hips, his lips tight. "So, I'm damned no matter what," he concluded. "Because you *are* pregnant. Yet if you hadn't been, you wouldn't have collapsed and I wouldn't have come here in the first place and realized what I *do* want."

Her knees finally gave up and she sank down on the arm of the couch. The leather creaked, a sound so cozy and comfortable that it seemed to make the ache inside her even worse.

"If you're worried that you won't get to see the baby, don't be."

"Would you forget about the baby for a minute?" His teeth practically snapped off each word.

She pressed her palm against her belly, feeling a hard thump from the baby in question. "How, Alex? How do I do that?"

He exhaled sharply, shoving his hands through his hair, making the short waves stand in spikes. "I don't know. How do I convince you of something I have no way of proving?"

"There's nothing to prove."

"Isn't there?"

The impasse existed between them, as alive and present as the baby anxiously moving inside her.

"How does Hunt figure into this?"

She wanted to weep. "I've told you. He doesn't!"

"You *slept* with him. Of all the women I know, you're the least likely to indulge in casual sex."

His voice was tight, but matter-of-fact, and it sent her flying off the edge. "It was fifteen minutes and the biggest mistake of my life!"

"Then *why?*"

"Because I couldn't have *you!*" Her breath was clawing at her lungs. Humiliation threatened to swamp her. She turned, wanting only to get away from him, from the deep foolishness of her own actions, and nearly fell face-first into the empty tub.

Alex caught her as she struggled for balance, and inserted himself between her and the danger. "You have to be careful."

She burst into tears.

He swore and lifted her off her feet.

"I don't need to be carried." The words hiccuped out of her.

"Shut up." He rounded the couch and went into the bedroom, settling her in the center of the bed.

She rolled away from him, but he came down after

her, halting her movements by clamping one of his legs over hers and dragging her half-beneath him.

"Be still."

She went still. Not because of his autocratic order, but because of the obvious part of him pressed against her hip that told her he wasn't only furious.

He was aroused.

"Yeah," he said gruffly. "It's a problem, what you do to me."

She looked away, closing her eyes. Tears burned beneath her lids, but her trembling didn't come from the tears. It was because of *him*.

Everything was because of him.

He sighed mightily, a man on the edge of his patience. "Nothing about this situation is perfect," he finally said slowly. "But it's what we've got. What does it matter how we got to this point? I want you with me. Your baby deserves a father. We could be good together, Nikki, and you know it. Just because you're afraid doesn't mean—"

Her head whipped around. "I'm not afraid of anything!" Fine words. If only they were true.

"Then prove it."

Her lips parted. She barely realized her tears had stopped. "Prove that I'm not afraid by agreeing to marry someone who doesn't love me? Marriage is surely hard enough without having such low expectations."

"Do you love me?" he demanded swiftly. "No. You're still in love with a kid who died *years* ago!"

"I am—" Realizing her mistake the moment the words flew out of her lips, she broke off.

His expression softened a little, though he couldn't possibly have known the confession she'd been about to make. "Marry me, Nikki," he said quietly. "Forget about the past for now. Forget about my cousin and let me take care of you and your baby."

Temptation was too quick to flood her veins. She actually hesitated. Had to force the words past her lips. "It wouldn't be right."

He lifted a hand and slowly drew her hair away from where it clung to her wet cheek. "Why not?"

"I…" She couldn't form the words that would explain why not. Couldn't seem to form a coherent sentence, for that matter.

Not when he was looking at her with those chocolate-brown eyes, so steadily. So…Alex.

But not quite the Alex she thought she'd known.

Which one was real?

The workaholic CEO?

The jean-clad man who sat on a bed and ate apples and peanut butter, and who ordered up a sleigh ride simply to please her?

"I don't know what to do. I've *always* known what to do."

"Don't think with your head. Lead from your heart."

"Those don't sound like words *you'd* ever follow."

His lips twisted a little. He stroked her hair back from her face, smoothing it over the velvet spread. "First time I followed my heart, I founded Huffington."

She was weakening. She could feel it inside of her— an inviting fissure that yawned wider and wider, enticing all the sensible reasons why she should *not* weaken to fall right in and dissolve. "If that was the first time, was there a second?"

His lids lowered a little, which seemed to make the appeal of his dark eyes even more concentrated. More heady. "Staying here with you."

Her throat tightened. "Don't tell me things that aren't true, Alex. I can't bear it."

"I've never lied to you, Nikki. Not when you worked for me. Not now. Not ever."

And that was the thing. Alex *wasn't* a liar. He wasn't manipulative. He was just...Alex.

His large palm cradled her head. His thumb smoothed from her temple down her cheek, taking away the remains of her tears. He lowered his head, his eyes still locked on hers. "Marry me."

The baby moved in a long, lazy flutter.

Alex's gaze finally left hers. He looked down to where he was half covering her, and she realized he must have felt the baby's movement, too.

His hand left her head and he pressed it flat against her belly, fingers splayed, encompassing and warm.

A moment later, the baby moved again, directly beneath his palm. "Amazing." His voice was soft. Awed.

The fissure expanded, cracking wide open.

"All right," she whispered. "Yes. I'll marry you."

Chapter Fourteen

"Home sweet home," Alex said when Nikki unlocked the front door of her town house in Cheyenne.

She looked at him over her shoulder and smiled.

She'd been hiding the tangle of nerves inside her for almost a week, ever since he'd proposed and she'd accepted. Particularly since her appointment with Dr. Carmichael that very morning, when he'd pronounced her fit and well enough to travel home.

A whole four days earlier than he'd originally predicted.

"I still advise you to be somewhat cautious with your diet and activities, but for the most part, you can get your life back to normal," he'd said, and his eyes had been amused, since he'd obviously been referring to the more intimate variety of "normal," about which it appeared both she and Alex had separately questioned him.

Alex, of course, had immediately arranged a charter flight home at the news that she was well enough to travel.

She hadn't been surprised.

Yes, she'd agreed to marry him, but she still needed to be practical about matters. He'd taken too much time away from Huffington because of her. Naturally, he'd wanted to return immediately. He'd made a good dozen phone calls before their arrival. She'd only made one. To Belle, to let her know they were coming home.

Now Alex ran his hands from her shoulders down her arms. "You okay?"

Again, she nodded. Managed a smile. She couldn't afford to kid herself that, back on his regular turf, he would continue focusing his considerable attention solely on her. "Just a little tired."

"I'll bet." He leaned past her, pushing the door wider. "Get inside. It's cold."

She let him hustle her through the door.

Everything about the town house—from the narrow entry table with its matching antique buffet lamps, to the slightly dusty cherrywood dining table at the opposite end—felt entirely unfamiliar.

"Smells a little musty in here." Alex set down her suitcase. "Need to crack open a window or two."

He was right, of course. The home she'd been able to purchase because of the very reasonable salary she'd once earned from him didn't smell bad, it just smelled as if it had been left abandoned for too long.

She dropped her keys in the little glass bowl she kept on the entry table for just that purpose, and ignored the cardboard box filled with mail that her neighbor had obviously continued bringing in for her, even when she hadn't returned home after that first week away.

"You can just leave the suitcase here," she told Alex. But he was already moving past her, heading straight for the open staircase that led up to her bedroom, as if he knew exactly where it would be even though he'd never once stepped foot in her home.

She walked to the kitchen. The plants in the greenhouse window over the sink were in desperate need of water, and she mindlessly pulled out her small watering can, shoved it under the faucet and flipped on the water.

"You've got a nice place." Alex walked up behind her, looping his hands around her waist. "Decorate it yourself?"

She carefully shut off the water, trying to ignore how utterly good it felt to be touched by him. "Yes. That's what those magazines I used to read on my lunch hour were for." She lifted the watering can and leaned forward a little to reach the plants.

His hands tightened on her hips and she realized too late the error of her ways. Leaning forward to water the plants had only succeeded in nudging her rear back against him.

"Gotta love those plants," he murmured, taking full advantage of her strategic misstep. His palms slipped boldly beneath her top, cradling her belly for a heart-breaking moment before they moved upward, arrowing straight for her breasts.

She trembled and water splashed on the window, pouring onto the pretty tiled surface instead of the parched plants. She quickly set the watering can down, her hands closing desperately over the edge of the sink before her knees simply dissolved. "Alex…"

His devilish fingers danced over her bra, then slid away. He pulled his hands from beneath her sweater, leaving her feeling contrarily bereft. He squeezed her shoulders, then brushed her hair away from the nape of her neck and kissed her there.

She nearly bit her tongue.

"I know you're tired," he murmured, lifting his head and sliding his arms around her, tugging her back against him. "You need food. Rest."

She stared blindly out the window.

"A night in your own bed." His deep voice dropped even further. "If you want it to be alone tonight, Nikki, just say so." His hands ran down her arms until they covered her white knuckles. "I do have some control. We'll have plenty of time to be together."

Together. Her eyes burned. From disbelief or relief that they'd have that time?

She still wasn't sure.

She turned in his arms, sliding her hands behind his neck. "And I don't seem to have *any* control," she admitted, her voice husky.

He inhaled slowly. Exhaled even more slowly. "Now?"

"Yes." Her head spun a little. "Upstairs. My bedroom."

He lifted her off her feet until their mouths were level. "Wrap your legs around my waist."

She obeyed.

He turned and walked out of the kitchen. Strode to the stairs. Took them easily, despite her weight, and went straight into her bedroom and placed her oh-so-deliberately in the center of her pristine, white, goose-down comforter. Then he straightened and pulled his sweater over his head, tossing it aside.

Nikki's mouth went dry. Her heart climbed up into her throat. He was so impossibly beautiful to her. He pulled off his boots, straightened yet again and undid the top button on his jeans. She pushed herself up on her elbows, vaguely shocked at her own avid attention as he popped free the second button on his fly. "Hurry up," she whispered.

"No. This time I set the rules, remember?"

How could she forget? His promise had been circling inside her head for days....

But when he reached the third button, they both went still as a chime rang through the town house.

"Is that—"

"My doorbell." She swallowed. Alex's distinctive silver BMW had been waiting for them in the executive lot at the airport when their chartered flight had landed. It now was parked at the curb in front of her town house. "Whoever it is will go away."

But the chime came again, demanding. And she frowned, sitting bolt upright when they heard the sound of her front door opening.

"Nikki? Honey, where are you?"

Disbelief flattened her. "Belle, I'm going to strangle her," she muttered under her breath. "I'll be down in a second, Mom," she yelled back hurriedly.

Unholy amusement crinkled Alex's eyes and he raised his eyebrows.

"Get dressed," she hissed, scooting off the bed.

"You're not sixteen," he reminded her.

"No," she allowed, racing out of the bedroom as if she were and had just been caught with a verboten boy in her room, rather than the man her family undoubtedly had all heard was supposed to be marrying her. The doorknob slipped out of her nervous hand and the door slammed. She raked back her hair and hurried to the steps, just as her mother and stepfather walked in.

"Hi." She grabbed the banister and hurried down to meet them.

"Honey, go careful," Gloria chided. "It's too easy to trip and fall."

The Clay contingent hadn't finished arriving, apparently, and Nikki froze midway down the stairs as she watched every single one of her five stepbrothers and their wives troop through her door.

"Maggie fell on the stairs when she was pregnant." That came from Daniel, the middle stepbrother. "Scared the living sh—life out of me."

Bringing up the rear were Belle and Cage, and it was her twin's gaze that Nikki managed to catch.

Belle smiled slightly and shrugged, mouthing a

"sorry" as she turned and closed the door. Her thick brown hair swung around her shoulders in a gleaming sheaf. She looked just what she was—an extremely happy new bride.

And for a moment, Nikki envied Belle that, even though she knew her sister and Cage had had no small amount of difficulties in reaching their happiness together.

"We brought food," Gloria said unnecessarily, because it was pretty obvious that everyone was carrying a dish of some sort.

Nikki was painfully aware of Alex still upstairs in her bedroom. "I see that. Um, what are you all doing here?" Her voice was about an octave too high, and she ignored the arch look Belle sent her. "I, um, I didn't expect a visit so soon."

"We came to see for ourselves that our girl was okay," Squire said. He might have been into his seventies now, but his iron-gray hair was as thick as his sons' and his blue gaze just as sharp. And that gaze was definitely looking speculatively behind Nikki.

She resolutely refused to turn around to see if Alex had appeared, and quickly descended the rest of the stairs. She hugged her mom first. "I guess Belle must've spilled the beans that we were on our way back." She'd spoken with her sister while Alex was arranging the charter.

"And we all headed straight down here to see," Gloria said comfortably. She tilted Nikki's head back and eyed her for a moment. Tsking. "Why, oh, why didn't you let any of us know what was going on?"

Nikki lifted her shoulders. What had seemed like a

bright idea then seemed ridiculously childish in the face of her mother's gentle chiding. "How was the cruise?"

"Too damn long," Squire complained, dropping a kiss on her head and hugging her before passing her on to the next arrivals—Tristan and his wife, Hope—and heading toward the kitchen with the box in his hands. "But your mama looks mighty fine in a bathing suit, so I managed to survive."

"Survived flirting with all the young women who did look fine in their bathing suits," Gloria corrected, laughing. She shooed everyone with a brush of her hands. "Come on now, there are too many of us to stand around here. Take the food on into the kitchen. Nikki, you sit yourself down and put up your feet. I'm glad that doctor in Montana saw fit to let you come home, but you're still looking peaked to me. Rebecca, what do you think?"

Nikki found herself maneuvered onto her big couch. Rebecca—a doctor in Weaver and married to Sawyer, who was the oldest of Nikki's stepbrothers—leaned over Nikki, her eyes narrowed humorously. "Frankly," she murmured, "I think she looks a little flushed."

Nikki's gaze slid toward the stairs.

Alex was coming down, looking as urbane as he ever did, and certainly not as though he'd just been stripping off his clothes in her bedroom.

All the chatter that had filled her town house ceased, and all eyes turned to her former boss.

And she knew she was blushing for certain.

Of all people to speak up, Cage, Nikki's only brother-in-law, did, though he generally was the last to speak in a crowd. He stuck out his hand. "Alex. Good to see you. Hear congratulations are in order."

Alex came down the last step and shook Cage's hand. "Thanks. How's Lucy?"

"Back to dancing." Cage didn't quite smile. "The staff at Huffington was really great to my daughter when she was treated after her riding accident."

"I'm glad to hear it."

"So." Belle's gaze slid between Nikki and Alex. "Have you set a date?"

Nikki quailed a little as everyone's attention—including Alex's—now turned to her. "Um, not yet."

"Well, there's plenty of time to talk about that in the next few days," Gloria said comfortingly. "But right now, the lasagna and pizza are getting cold. So let's eat."

Nikki preferred to stay out of the stampede, so she sat right where she was on the couch. Alex and Cage, still talking, hung toward the back. In minutes, Squire's sons—Sawyer, Daniel, Matthew and Jefferson—had all joined the little tête-à-tête.

Lord only knew what sort of grilling Alex was getting.

Hope, who was the youngest of the Clay wives and only a few years older than Nikki and Belle, sat down on the couch beside her. She folded her hands over her own pregnant belly. "You're a month further along than I am," she complained lightly. "So how come I look twice the size of you?"

Tristan worked his way around the couch and handed Hope a paper plate nearly overflowing with pepperoni pizza. "Maybe you're carrying twins," he said, looking alternately pleased and horrified at the idea.

"Bite your tongue," Hope said severely. But her violet eyes were twinkling behind her glasses.

"I'll leave that for you," Tristan murmured.

Emily, who had been married the longest of any of the sisters-in-law, scooted in beside Nikki. She'd been raised since childhood alongside Tristan, for Squire had taken her in when her parents died. "Get a room," she drawled, eyeing her brother-in-law. "Or better yet, try to control yourself. Hope's already knocked up again."

"Shut up, Em. We've all heard that Leandra walked in on you and Jefferson the other day. Playing doctor in the middle of the afternoon? Where's your control, girl?"

Nikki shot Emily a look, and sure enough, the other woman was blushing.

"Don't let Jefferson hear you," Emily hissed. "The poor man wanted to die. And Lee didn't really catch us—you know—in flagrante. Thank God. She's only eleven, but she's growing up way too fast." Emily nudged Nikki's arm. "You just wait until that one—" she nodded at Nikki's belly "—forgets what a closed door is supposed to mean."

Nikki's front door hadn't just been closed, it had been locked, as well. And that hadn't stopped her family from coming right on in. She realized she was looking over at Alex again, and studiously turned away, afraid she might be caught drooling or something, and *never* hear the end of it. "Speaking of Leandra," she murmured, desperate to change the subject, "where are the kids?" There were currently eleven, ranging from Ryan—Sawyer and Rebecca's—at sixteen, to Hope and Tristan's youngest, Erik, at five.

"Ryan and Lucy are riding herd on them all at the ice-skating rink." Hope smiled, looking sympathetic. "Bec, Emily, Maggie and I insisted to the guys that there was no way we were descending on you, unannounced like this, with that horde in tow, as well."

Nikki always enjoyed seeing her nieces and nephews. But at the moment, she was grateful for a little less confusion reigning supreme in her home. It was already bulging at the seams with the adults. Toss in nearly a dozen rambunctious children, teens and near-teens, and—

Well. Her mind simply refused to wrap around it.

Squire joined them, a plate balanced on his large palm. He sat down on the coffee table across from Nikki and, like magic, Hope, Emily and Tristan all hurried away.

Cowards. Judging by the look on Squire's face, they didn't want to be around to hear whatever the man had to say.

Frankly, just then Nikki wished she had the nerve to skedaddle, herself.

He didn't waste time. "Good thing your mother is pretty much a saint. Or she might have tried putting you over her knee for keeping what happened in Montana from everyone." His sharp gaze rested on Nikki's face and his gruff voice lowered. "Fact is, I sorta felt a desire to do that myself. I love you like my own and you know it. But twenty-seven or not, child, you worry your mom like that again, and you'll answer to me."

"And you'll answer to me if you upset Nikki," Alex said evenly.

Nikki started, her head jerking up. Alex was standing right behind her, and his hand closed over her shoulder as if he knew just how near she was to fleeing and damning the consequences.

"What's done is done," he added. "Nik had her reasons, and you all can see for yourselves that she and the baby are doing well now. I'm going to keep it that way."

Squire slowly set his plate aside. He didn't stand. Just looked over Nikki's head at Alex, his expression clearly one of the sizing-up variety.

Nikki didn't need her master's degree to know what conclusions her stepfather was drawing. What they all were thinking. They all wanted to know why Alex had taken so long to do right by her and the child he'd fathered. That's just the way they were.

And she wanted to stand up and scream that of all people, Alex had done nothing wrong, and that she loved them all deeply, but would they just go and leave them alone?

Of course, she did none of those things.

She sat there, silent as an abashed child, while the baby inside her pitched and rolled, seeming to want to express all the frustration Nikki couldn't.

After an interminable silence that was only more obvious for being underscored by the cacophony of voices around them, Squire's lips quirked. "Okay, then," he said with a faint nod. He picked up his plate once more.

His eyes were twinkling a little. "Better eat up," he advised, half under his breath. "Sooner the food's gone, the sooner those boys of mine'll start herding their wives home again."

Then, as if he'd been merely passing the time of day over pepperoni and mushrooms, rather than coming to some conclusion that evidently satisfied him, he headed into the kitchen. "Emily," he commented in an aggrieved good-ol'-boy tone, "when are you gonna get that son of mine to cut his hair? I swear, I can't tell Jefferson from Leandra sometimes."

Nikki bit the inside of her lip. As long as she'd known Squire, he'd complained about Jefferson's long hair. Privately, she figured he'd be the first one put out if his middle son ever did whack off his wrist-thick blond ponytail any shorter than his shoulders.

Alex rounded the couch and sat beside her. He propped his boot on the edge of her coffee table, seemingly as comfortable doing so as her relatives were. "You have a good family."

She did. And he did not. "I think they're pretty okay," she murmured.

"You know what they're thinking, though."

She dipped her chin. If she cared less for her family, she'd just tell them all the whole miserable, pathetic truth. That she'd slept with a man she shouldn't have because she knew she'd never have the man she really wanted. Instead, she was a coward. And she was letting Alex shoulder the blame.

"I'm sorry," she whispered. He closed his hand over

hers, which she hadn't even realized were twisted tightly together in her lap.

"You need to relax." He ran his thumb over her white knuckles. "Or the blood pressure you finally got down is going to be right back where it was. I don't think you want to spend more mandatory time off your feet."

Relax. Easier said than done. "Don't want that," she agreed, feelingly. "Once was more than enough."

He made a soft sound. Agreement, she supposed. Then he squeezed her hand a little. "I'm gonna go. You've got enough people around here as it is."

He was the one person she didn't want to leave, yet she forced her lips into a smile and nodded. "You'll probably head straight to Huffington."

He neither confirmed nor denied it. But she knew him. He'd stayed away from the office—physically, at least—for too long.

Because of her.

It was still unfathomable.

Was he already regretting it?

She watched him weave his way through the throng that was her family, telling them good-night.

He didn't even bother putting on his coat, just grabbed it up on his way out the door.

And then he was gone.

"Well." Belle plopped down on the couch beside her. She slung her arm over Nikki's shoulders. "So you're marrying the boss. Who'd have thunk it?"

There were so many times when she and Belle were

on the same wavelength, sharing thoughts without having to say a word. The twin connection.

It seemed to be absent at that moment, though.

And it was just another yawning emptiness inside her, like the abyss she felt yearning for Alex.

Her eyes burned. She swallowed. Pushed herself awkwardly out of the deep, overstuffed couch. She had no idea why she'd ever purchased the thing. It was made to accommodate a person much taller than herself. A person like Alex.

"Excuse me," she mumbled hurriedly as she went to the door.

She stopped on the porch steps, calling his name.

He turned, obviously surprised. "What's wrong? You should be resting."

Her breath seemed locked in her chest, and it had nothing to do with the winter temperature. She took a few steps toward him. "Are you sure?"

He strode the rest of the way back to her and flipped his coat around her shoulders. "Sure about what?"

"Getting married."

"Yes."

"Will you come back here after you've been to the office?"

His smile was slow and full of promise. "Yes."

Chapter Fifteen

She was wrapped in a long robe when Alex returned from the office hours later.

There were no cars or pickup trucks congesting the street in front of her town house. Her family had all departed.

Considering it was nearly midnight, he wasn't surprised.

He *was* surprised, however, that she was still awake.

Awake and waiting.

Her hair was wrapped in a towel that was much better designed for soaking up water than the robe, which clung to her very damp body.

She wore virginal white, but she looked…womanly. Ripe.

And his control where she was concerned had long ago gone out the window. "Were you in the bath?"

"Shower," she admitted. "I wanted to wash off the traveling, and...relax. I didn't hear the bell, at first."

He'd rung it several times. Had felt a distinct chill when she hadn't immediately answered.

"Why aren't you relaxed?"

She flushed.

"Are you going to let me in?"

Her lashes dipped. And even though she'd made it more than plain that she wanted him to return, she seemed to have a death grip on the lapels of her robe, holding them tightly closed at the base of her neck, which only pulled the shimmering white fabric more tightly over her breasts. She had a death grip on the doorknob, as well.

He could see that her knuckles were white. He reached out and caught a drop of water near her chin with his thumb. "What's the matter?"

Color bloomed in her cheeks. "Nothing."

He covered her knuckles with his palm. "What?"

She swallowed. Took a step back and pulled the door wider, allowing him inside. "They've all left."

"I figured." He gently tugged the door free from her grasp and pushed it shut. "Have you changed your mind?"

She let go of her robe finally, only to dash her hand across her damp forehead. "I thought you had."

"I'm not going to change my mind. Not about making love to you. Not about marrying you. Raising the baby."

"My mother wanted to know where we would do it."

Nikki flushed a little. "Get married, I mean." The flowing length of her robe seemed to float around her legs for a moment. Without her holding them together, the lapels revealed a narrow wedge of skin from the base of her throat downward.

"Doesn't matter to me. Wherever you want." As long as it happened.

They were still standing in the foyer, and the only light came from the two small lamps on the narrow table next to him.

"I need a towel. I'm dripping water everywhere."

"I like you wet," he said pointedly.

She caught her breath at that. He heard the faint catch, saw the rise of her breasts beneath the slick, clinging robe. The narrow wedge became a little wider. He could see the shadow between her breasts. He reached forward. Slowly caught the end of the sash with his fingers.

She looked up at him, her eyes wide, her lips parted softly.

He pulled on the sash. The bow she'd tied slid free. "There's nobody, nothing to stop us this time. Except you," he murmured.

Her long, lovely throat worked in a deep swallow. Then she lifted her hand to the towel twisted around her head, and pulled it free. Her hair looked like twisting strands of brown fire as it tumbled around her shoulders. A drop of water hit his hand and he was vaguely surprised it didn't sizzle. He took a few steps and sat on her big couch. He still held the sash, and she turned with him, standing in front of him.

When he tugged again, the sash slid free, slithering out of the two loops meant to hold it in place. The robe parted a few inches, revealing the high swell of her abdomen.

Want screamed through him with the speed of a freight train. He dropped the sash and tucked a none-too-steady index finger beneath the robe, drawing the slick fabric aside as if unwrapping the rarest of treasures. And inch by inch, he slowly revealed her. Full, taut.

So achingly beautiful he couldn't look away even when he saw the peach blush tinge her creamy skin. It crept down her throat, bloomed over her breasts. And as he watched, he saw the baby move.

He stared. She pressed her hand to the spot near her navel. "I—"

He drew her hand away. "Does it hurt?" His gaze was glued to her abdomen, anticipation roaring inside him. Only it wasn't purely sexual. It was…more. He'd deliberately put away any likelihood of having a family of his own. And now, not only did he want Nikki and this child, but he was beginning to realize he might want even more. He hadn't changed his decision for Val even when she'd been desperate after her miscarriage. But now he was considering changing everything. Because of Nikki.

And it scared the life out of him.

Her fingers curled over his. "No, it doesn't hurt. Not this time, anyway."

Another visible thump. "Look at that."

She made a soft sound. He slanted a look up to her face. "It's one thing to, um, to see me the way you have before." She'd been mostly clothed when they'd been intimate. "It's another to…" She trailed off.

"You're amazing, Nikki," he murmured. "You…look amazing."

Her eyes darkened even more, appearing nearly black in the gentle light from the foyer lamps.

He pressed his palm over hers, which still covered the place where the baby had kicked.

She was trembling.

He lifted his other hand, cradling her belly, her baby, her. "And I've never wanted a woman as much as I want you right now." He sat forward and pressed his mouth to the center of her stomach, right above her navel.

Beneath his hand, her fingers curled, then slid away, only to settle, hesitantly, on his shoulder. "I look in the mirror sometimes and don't even recognize myself," she admitted softly.

"You're always beautiful." He kissed her smooth skin. Tasted her navel. Felt the shudder work through her when his hands moved farther, settling on her slender hips, slipping behind her back, edging her closer to him. "And I can't remember what it was like not to want you." He pressed his mouth to her abdomen again, open, hot, his control increasingly nebulous.

Her hand sank into his hair, flexing against his scalp like a greedy cat.

He rose suddenly, his hands skimming up her spine, dragging down the robe. It slid off her shoulders, clung for an instant to her damp skin, then drifted to the floor, reminding him of when he'd watched and waited that first night in the cabin for the bedspread to fall off the foot of the bed.

Nearly blind with need, want, he caught her head in his hands, lifting her lips to his. She kissed him back, the soft sound she made filling his mouth. Her hands sneaked between them, fumbling with the buttons on his shirt, finally just yanking the shirttails free.

His control snapped. Her mouth clung to his as he tore off his shirt, kicked off his boots and dragged at his belt. The sound of her gasping breaths spurred him. He finally caught her up against him, lifting her right off the floor, skin to skin, breast to chest. She moaned his name, her arms twining around his shoulders, her wet hair clinging to him as well as her.

"Have to slow down," he muttered, as much a reminder to himself as to her. But he didn't slow. He pulled her over him, sinking down on the couch, and felt all that glorious wet heat graze over him. More than tantalizing, more than enticing. He needed to be inside her more than he needed air.

"Now," she gasped, her breath warm on his neck. "Now, Alex, oh, please."

He caught her hips, lifting them. Pulled her back down, sinking deep.

She cried out, her fingernails digging into his shoulders. He barely felt them. His own fingers were tangled in her hair, and he arched up into her, baptizing himself in the fire that was Nikki.

She trembled like a wild thing. Gave everything she was, unstinting and generous, a match where he'd never before felt matched, and he knew that no matter how many times he made love to her, he would spend the rest of his life never having enough.

Her body tightened around him, his name a soft, keening sound on her lips, again and again. Like quick-silver, he felt his soul rising inside him. And then he felt more: the ripples that tore her apart and spun her back together. A rough sound ripped out of him as he poured himself into her, an endless aching pulse driven by the heart inside her.

And when they finally collapsed against each other, a tangle of long, wet hair, shaking legs and clutching arms, he realized with some dim portion of his mind that instead of feeling emptied, for the first time in his life he felt filled.

Shudders were still quaking through her, gentler now. And impossibly, he felt himself hardening all over again.

"Oh," she whispered, obviously aware. "Alex."

He groaned. His legs were weak. His lungs felt like he'd run a marathon.

He felt reborn.

He carefully disentangled them, even though it was about as easy as cutting out his heart. He managed to get to his feet, and pulled her up with him. "This time," he said, forming the words with some difficulty, "bed." Her bed.

Her lips curved softly, as if she'd just been given a fresh dose of adrenaline. Casting a glance at him over her shoulder, a look full of promise, she walked over to the stairs and slowly ascended them.

He caught up to her before she made it to the landing, and slid his arm around her, stopping her progress long enough to press his lips to her shoulder. To drag his hands over her breasts. To cradle the swell of her baby. To delve downward, to where she was soft and swollen and heated. For him. From him.

He groaned, so greedy for more that he could have taken her right then and there, standing on the step. And she seemed to know it, the little witch, for she arched her back, pressing her shapely bottom against his rigid length even as she caught his wrist between her fingers, holding his hand intimately against her.

He spun her around suddenly, glad of the fact that he could surprise her, and lifted her off her feet, hustling up the remaining three steps. "Bed."

She laughed a little, a breathless sound of eagerness and yearning that went to his head faster than any liquor ever could. In her bedroom, he ripped back the comforter. Pillows flew everywhere.

Then he bore her down in the center, and she folded her arms around him, her hips cradling his, wordlessly offering.

He sank inside her.

And again it seemed that everything he'd ever wanted in this world flooded through him.

The soft bleat of a phone woke Nikki.

She sat up, focusing on the sound for a moment before she recognized it as Alex's cell phone.

The phone was downstairs. Where his clothes still were.

Sunlight filled the room. She'd hadn't bothered to close the drapes, simply because Alex hadn't given her a moment to think of such mundane matters as they'd made love, again and again, until dawn slid its silvery fingers through the window.

He murmured something and wrapped his arm, warm and possessive, around her waist, pulling her close again.

No contest.

The phone would stop ringing, eventually.

She lay back down next to him, greedily taking in the view. His hair was rumpled. His cheeks were bristled. His face was relaxed.

The phone beeped again.

Imperious.

Alex still didn't move.

The alarm clock on the nightstand shouted the fact that it was after ten.

She carefully moved his arm and slid off the bed.

He rolled over, burying his head in her pillow.

Her heart squeezed and she quickly, silently, left the bedroom before whoever his impatient caller was could wake him.

Downstairs, his clothes were still strewn across the living room, and she snatched up his shirt, tugging it over her shoulders as she hunted for the ringing phone. She finally found it in the pocket of his coat and flipped it open.

"Hello?"

"I'm looking for Alex Reed." The voice was tentative, but Nikki would have recognized it even without the caller ID readout.

"Miriam? This is Nikki."

She could practically feel Miriam relax a little. "Oh, thank heavens. Nikki, where *is* Alex? I know he was in the office last night because he left me a massive amount of notes. He has a new administrative assistant who's starting today, and Mr. Reed *Senior,* is here."

Alarm skittered down Nikki's spine. She started gathering up Alex's clothing. His pants. His gold cuff links. "Alex's father?"

"Yes. He's been here for an hour and he refuses to leave. He says Mr. Reed needs to stop hiding, and that he's going to own Huffington before he's finished. Everyone's in an uproar. Mr. Reed doesn't *hide* from anyone!" Her voice went indignant. "Do you have any idea where he is?"

Nikki had already started up the steps. "Don't worry. Give him a few minutes, and he'll be at the office."

She folded the phone, disconnecting the call, and hurried into the bedroom, where Alex was still sleeping, sprawled across her bed as if he owned it. She sat beside him and gently shook his shoulder. "Alex. Wake up."

One deep brown eye slitted open. His lips started to curve. "I like you in my shirt," he murmured, his voice husky with sleep.

She felt a glow of pleasure at that. "Miriam called. Your father's at Huffington."

His half smile died. "*At* Huffington."

Nikki nodded and dropped his clothes on the bed. "Evidently he's got the staff in quite a state. I'll make you some coffee while you shower. You can drink it on the way."

Amazingly, he smiled again. "Feeling a little bossy this morning, are you?"

She blushed. "I…"

He tugged on the shirttail covering her thigh, pulling her closer. "I'm teasing." He sat up. Pressed a hard kiss to her lips and, in one smooth move, slid his shirt from her shoulders and dragged his gaze over her for a lingering moment. Then he was heading to her bathroom, his somewhat rumpled clothes hooked in his hand.

Nikki wasted a few precious minutes sitting there, shaking from that look of his, then gathered her wits about her and shrugged into a loose T-shirt and a pair of fleecy sweatpants and went down to make the coffee.

When he came downstairs a short while later, his hair was gleaming wet and slick, his jaw still unshaven. His shirt looked a little worse for wear, given the wrinkles in it and the missing button midway down. He hadn't bothered with his cuff links, nor had he bothered tucking in the tails, and there was something incredibly intimate about that fact.

Which was silly.

Hadn't they been as intimate as two people could possibly be?

Still, her hand trembled a little as she fit the lid on an insulated coffee mug. "Why would your father actually *come* to Cheyenne? Could he be recanting his intention to acquire Macfield and Huffington?"

Alex shook his head and shrugged into his coat. "Only thing that would bring my father to the land of the uncivilized—his words, not mine—is the opportunity to gloat."

She handed him the coffee. "Drive carefully."

Alex brushed his mouth over hers.

A moment later, he was gone.

She hugged herself. The town house seemed suddenly empty without Alex's vitality. She turned off the coffeemaker and padded back upstairs. The bed was tumbled, silently broadcasting that for the first time since she'd bought it, she hadn't been alone in it.

When she married Alex, would he expect her to live at the Echelon with him? Would he come here, to her place? Would they find something of their own? Together?

And why was she worrying about where they might live when he was on his way to meet his father? When he stood a very real chance of losing his life's work to a man he detested?

She hurried into the bathroom and flipped on the shower. The mirror was still edged with steam from Alex's shower when she stepped under the hot water.

Alex had stood by her when she couldn't even stand. It was time she started standing beside *him*.

"You don't own Huffington and you never will," Alex said flatly, watching his father pace back and forth inside his office. "Coming here, throwing your weight around as if you have a right, upsetting my staff, is not going to change anything."

Alex Sr. snorted. He stopped pacing long enough to

flick a disdainful glance out the window. In the light streaming in, his color looked high. "*Somebody* is going to own it. It might as well be me."

"I'd choose anyone over you."

"Macfield is mine. It's only a matter of crossing a few t's. You'll never find another company to take their place. If you don't keep expanding, you'll die. Face it, boy. You're between a rock and a hard place. You can't even go public, because you know RHS will be right there, waiting."

"I don't give a damn what RHS is doing. You're *not* going to pollute my company with one finger of yours. I'll close and lock every clinic door myself before I'll let that happen. And I'll make damn sure every single one of my employees finds work with *your* competition."

"High and mighty," Alex Sr. snapped. "Always thought you were above the rest of us. Too *good* to take your place in RHS."

"RHS wasn't the problem, Dad," Alex drawled. He sat on the edge of his desk, his arms at his sides. "You know that. It was *you.*"

"I *will* have what I want," Alex Sr. said through gritted teeth.

Alex studied his father for a moment. Beads of sweat stood out on the man's forehead, yet he didn't shrug out of his suit coat. God forbid. It might show some sign of weakness. "You need to retire, Dad. You're…what? Sixty-five years old now. Hell. Let Hunt have a chance at the chairman's seat for a while."

"I will *not* be put out to pasture!" The man's voice

rose. "Particularly by that whelp, who can't even keep his pants zipped."

Alex laughed suddenly. "Is that what this is about? Hunt's *finally* moving on the chairmanship?" He wouldn't have expected it of his cousin. Hunt didn't have that much ambition.

"The only thing Hunter moves on are women." Alex Sr. was practically shouting. "And the only thing you do is clean up after him. I hear you're doing it again. What's the matter with you, Son? Can't have a kid of your own, so you have to keep taking up with Hunter's tramps?"

"Excuse me."

Both men whipped around and looked at the doorway.

Nikki stood there. Her face was pale.

"Perhaps you should close the door for this discussion," she said evenly. "Your shouting can be heard down on the first floor."

"Who are *you?*" Alex Sr. demanded.

Alex started toward Nikki, stretched out his hand to her.

"I'm one of the tramps," she said stiffly. Her bruised gaze collided with his for a long moment.

And he knew she'd heard more than enough.

"Nik—"

She shook her head a little. Took a step back and closed his office door in his face.

Chapter Sixteen

"Can I stay here?" Nikki stood on the small porch of Belle and Cage's home at the Lazy-B.

Belle blinked away her shock at her twin's appearance and hurriedly pushed open the glass storm door. "What's wrong?"

Nikki swallowed. "Everything," she whispered. "He lied."

Her sister's eyebrows drew together. "Who? Alex?"

Nikki nodded.

Belle tsked. "You told me Alex never lies." She closed the door and herded her to one of the old-fashioned chairs that filled the small living room.

"I was wrong." Nikki opened her hand, and found the car keys clenched in her fist had left indentations.

She looked dully around her. "Where are Cage and Lucy?" It was nearly dinnertime. She'd driven straight from Huffington to the Lazy-B.

"Lucy's spending the night in Weaver with her friend, Anya. Cage'll be in soon." Belle crouched in front of Nikki's chair, holding her hands. "What happened? Last night, you and Alex looked like you could barely keep away from each other, even with the family around."

"Family." Nikki swallowed. "I should have paid more attention to Valerie. She came to Lucius, you know. To see Alex. She certainly didn't expect to see me." Nikki rested her hand on her belly. "Especially this way. She even said it. *They never are.*"

Belle rubbed her forehead. "What?"

"I told Val the baby wasn't Alex's. And she said 'They never are.' I just let it slide by." She shook her head. How stupid she was.

"If the baby isn't Alex's, then whose is it?" Belle's voice was calm.

Nikki's eyes burned. She'd managed not to cry during the drive from Cheyenne. "I've been so stupid, Annabelle."

Belle huffed a little and slid her arms around Nikki's shoulders. "You've never been stupid a day in your life," she declared.

"I let myself believe that he actually wanted *me*. Turns out, it really *was* just about the baby. I overheard his father. Alex can't have children."

"Did Alex say that?" Belle's question was careful.

"He didn't have to. I could see it in his eyes."

"Okay. You have to start at the beginning here, Nik, because I am totally lost."

Nik. The only other person besides Belle who called her that was Alex.

Nikki covered her face with her hands and cried.

"I think we should be waiting to do this," Belle said the next morning.

"Is that why you insisted on coming back to Cheyenne with me? To talk me out of packing?"

"You were awake most of the night crying," Belle said evenly. "I didn't think you should be driving."

Nikki dumped into a box an armload of clothing that she'd be lucky to ever fit into again. "I'm pregnant and unemployed. Should I just sit around here gestating until my town house is foreclosed on? No. It's better to get the thing on the market. Sell it before I lose it. Hope's old house in Weaver is still empty. I'll look for a job there. I'll stay there until I can afford another place of my own."

Belle sighed, clearly unhappy about the entire matter.

Nikki didn't care.

She needed to get out of Cheyenne, as far away from Alex as she could get.

She flipped the box closed and slapped packing tape over it, then moved on to the next drawer. She'd have to send Belle out to buy some more boxes before the morning was over. She'd only had a few in her closets, tidily saved from when she'd moved *into* the town house.

Too bad the boxes had Huffington Sports Clinic emblazoned on the sides.

She pushed herself to her feet and yanked down the hem of her shirt over her unfastened jeans.

She was back to her own clothes. Accepting her mother's offer of a shopping spree would be far, *far* easier than wearing Alex's jeans again.

Annoyed with her own thoughts, she flipped on the radio, turning the music up loud. If it was loud enough, would the voice in her head—*they never are, they never are*—be drowned out?

She went into the bathroom. Alex's gold cuff links sat on the edge of the sink. She picked them up, weighing the simple round discs in the palm of her hand. Alex was the only man she knew whose shirts—even everyday ones—required cuff links.

She abruptly set them down on the counter and snatched open a drawer, gathering up the contents. Brushes. Combs. Cosmetics. She dumped it all in the tote bag she dragged from beneath the sink, and then yanked the towels off the towel bar, only to realize she needed another box.

She left the towels heaped in the sink.

There was nothing neat and orderly about her packing, and she didn't care.

"Here." Belle came into the bedroom, her hand extended. "Your cell phone was in the kitchen garbage. It was ringing. Otherwise I wouldn't have noticed before I took the bag out to the Dumpster."

She should have turned it off before she'd pitched it. "I don't need it." After another month, she wouldn't be able to afford the monthly payment on it, anyway.

Belle looked a trifle impatient. "You're not throwing away a perfectly good cell phone just because you don't want to talk to Alex. For all you know, it could have been Mom calling you."

Nikki pushed a button, displaying the missed calls. Alex. Six times. "Mom has *not* called," she said flatly. "She's back at the Double-C, thinking that her grandchild isn't going to be born out of wedlock, after all."

Nikki turned off the phone and tossed it on the bare mattress.

Which only reminded her of the bedding that was still in her washing machine.

"Mom is *not* worried about that."

That was true. Gloria didn't operate that way, and Nikki felt childish for even having the thought.

Belle picked up the suitcase Nikki had used for her trip, and set it on the bed, flipping back the top. "Are these clothes clean or not? If they are, I can probably fit another drawerful of clothes in here. Save on a box."

Nikki reached over and plucked a familiar gray sweater out. Alex's. "They're clean," she said, and damned the fact that her voice was raw again. His cuff links and his sweater. She'd have to send them to him or something.

Though he would probably never even miss them.

A wave of tiredness sucked at her and she sat down on the side of the bed. It was considerably firmer than the round bed at the cabin.

The loud radio music morphed into chatter between two deejays. A commercial for the charity Valentine's Day ball sponsored by Huffington Sports Clinic followed.

Nikki blinked rapidly.

Belle rubbed her shoulder. "Maybe you should talk to him."

Nikki shook her head. She'd managed to convey the entire story to her twin the night before, after she'd exhausted one round of tears. "What for?"

"Give him a chance to explain."

"There's nothing to explain."

The deejays picked up their noisy chatter again. Belle sighed a little and leaned over to turn down the noise, but her hand paused when they both heard Alex's name mentioned.

"…lot of excitement at Huffington yesterday, and all of us here at K-country are sending Alex Reed our best thoughts."

Belle looked at Nikki, her eyebrows lifting. "What's that supposed to mean?"

"Shh."

"According to the hospital spokesman, cards and flowers should be sent to Huffington Sports Clinic. Again, that address is—"

Nikki shot to her feet. Belle was only a step behind her. "I'm driving," her sister said.

They had to stop at the information desk inside the hospital doors. "Alex Reed's room?"

The white-haired woman manning the desk consulted her computer. "He's not allowed visitors."

The anxious stone inside Nikki's stomach grew to a rock that steadily sank toward the ground. Belle grabbed her by the waist. "This is Mr. Reed's fiancée," she said firmly. "What room?"

The woman eyed Nikki's obviously pregnant person. "Third floor," she finally said. "Intensive Care."

Nikki's legs nearly dissolved. "I knew something like this would happen."

Belle's grip tightened on her waist. "What? The elevator's over there. Come on."

"It's Cody all over again."

Belle didn't stop moving. "This is *not* Cody," she said firmly. She jabbed the call button for the elevator.

"Alex was right when he said I was afraid." She stared at the elevator doors. They were dark bronze. Slightly reflective.

"You've never been afraid of anything," Belle chided softly.

"I lose every man I love," she whispered. "Dad. Cody."

"Alex?"

The voice that spoke was deep. Familiar.

Her eyes burned. She stared at the third form that joined their reflections, and felt the blood drain out of her head.

"Well, *you're* clearly not in ICU." Belle was the first to break the silence as they turned to see Alex standing behind them.

"My father," he said, his gaze steady on Nikki's face. "He had a heart attack yesterday afternoon. In my office."

Nikki swayed. Both Alex and Belle grabbed for her and she stiffened her knees. "I'm okay. How is he?"

Belle released her.

Alex did not. "He's holding his own. I've been trying to reach you. I was worried."

"I'm, uh, just going to go explore the gift shop. Or something. Anything," Belle murmured.

Nikki wanted to call her back, but her sister had already escaped across the corridor into the little gift shop. Nikki was left there with Alex.

Who looked terrible. For the first time ever, he seemed older than his years.

But despite his appearance, she couldn't help the relief that was flooding through her.

"I would have come after you if he hadn't collapsed. I would have explained."

There was no pretending she didn't know what he referred to. "It doesn't matter."

"Yes, it does." He cut off an oath when the elevator slid open behind them and a half-dozen people stepped out. "We can't talk here."

"We don't have to talk *any*where." He was okay. She was desperately grateful for that.

"Yes, we do." As if he had every right, he pushed open a door to a smoked-glass conference room and nudged her inside. "Sit."

She didn't want to sit. Assured of Alex's well-being, she just wanted to run. "Valerie was pregnant with Hunter's baby, too, wasn't she."

"Yes. Do you love me? Is that what you were going to say out there? You lost your dad. And Cody. And me?"

She had to press her lips together for a moment to

keep some semblance of composure. She was trembling. "How did your father know about me?"

"Where do you think Hunt got the money for that check he evidently gave you? And, no, I did not know about the check until my father brought up the subject in my office yesterday."

"He also said *you* can't have children."

"Can't and haven't are two different things. He thinks I can't because I had the mumps when I was young. I *haven't* because I had a vasectomy."

She swallowed. "A vasectomy?"

"I told you, I didn't particularly think I'd be a good parent. I *would* have told you."

"And I'm supposed to believe that?"

"You didn't want to tell me about Hunt," he reminded her flatly. "I made a mistake, okay? This is…new territory for me."

"There's *nothing* new about this," Nikki countered painfully. "This is just a repeat of Valerie."

"I hope to hell it isn't. She *lost* her baby, remember?"

Nikki's arm swept over her belly, protectively. "That's not what I meant."

"Despite the fact that I was disgusted with both Valerie and Hunter, I married her because I didn't want her going off the deep end. Hunt was married. He had no intention of leaving his wife for Valerie. She wasn't like you, Nik. She wasn't strong. Hell, she wasn't capable of getting through a hangnail without help from a drink, much less having a baby. I cared about her as much as I cared about anyone, but I was never in love with her, and when we split, it was a relief to us both. And I'm not going to let you use this as an excuse!"

Her jaw loosened. "An excuse for what?"

"Pushing me away because you're afraid. I heard you, Nik. I heard what you told Belle. But *I* am not going anywhere."

She swallowed. The need to sit in one of the thickly padded swivel chairs around the small table was strong. "You lied to me," she said, once she was sure her voice wouldn't crack. "And you told me you'd never lie to me."

"A lie by omission only. I *would* have told you."

"When?"

"Maybe after I adjusted to the fact that I'd fallen in love for the first damn time in my life—with a woman who'd made it plain she did *not* love *me!*"

Her knees gave up.

She sat.

Hope, where she hadn't expected any, bloomed warm and fierce inside her.

"I never said I didn't love you." Her voice was faint.

"You never said you did," he countered.

She couldn't look at him. "This is only because you want my child to be your child."

"Yes." He gritted his teeth and crouched before her, closing his hands over the arms of the chair, effectively trapping her in place. "I want *your* child to be my child. Because I love *you.* I love the way you believe in me. I love you enough that I'll have the reversal if you want to take that much of a chance on me. If you want to give *this* baby a brother or sister. But Nikki, if all I'd wanted was access to another Reed baby, I sure in hell wouldn't have gotten up close and personal with its mother. I'd have put the same lawyers on the situation that handled the other two children that Hunt carelessly sired."

"Other?"

"Yes. Other. He makes a habit of carelessness, Nik. Believe me. Valerie might have been the first, but she wasn't the only, and God help us, but you're probably not the last."

"Where are they?"

"Well provided for, both with parents who *do* love them, and thankfully, nowhere near the jackals that comprise the Reed clan. I sure didn't go chasing after those women to propose to *them.*"

"You could have explained all this."

"And give you another reason to realize why I'm not good enough to replace Cody in your heart?"

"Cody's only a memory in my heart," she whispered. "He was a boy I loved. And you…"

Alex waited, his expression tense. "Yes?"

She bit her lip. Took in a quick breath. "I thought I knew you," she whispered. "When I worked with you. I thought I knew everything there was to know about you. And I thought I loved that man. I did love that man."

His jaw clenched. "And now?"

"And now, after you stayed with me in Lucius when you didn't have to—"

"Don't give me gratitude, Nikki. That's not ever going to be enough."

"But I am grateful." She fumbled with her purse. Opened it and drew out his gray sweater, which she'd shoved inside. Her fingers sank into the soft knit. "If you hadn't come to Lucius, I would never have met the rest of you. The man beyond the CEO."

His brow knit. "Makes me sound like I have multiple personalities," he muttered.

"No." She lifted her hand and rested it on that tight, pulsing jaw. "Just one. One man. Who is so much more than I ever gave him credit for. I loved Cody, yes. But I never needed him. I never *needed* anyone the way I need you, until I fell in love with you—the whole you—in that cabin in Montana. And you're right. I'm scared to death of losing you." She sucked in an unsteady breath. "Because I don't think I could survive it. I was so scared today when we heard the news on the radio and I thought something had happened to you. It didn't matter how hurt I was. I had to know, to see for myself that you were…were—"

"Fine," he finished. He caught her head between his hands, his fingers sliding into her hair. "But *I'm* scared to death you'll realize what kind of family you're marrying into, and head for the hills. And you know me. I don't *get* scared. The only times I've ever felt that are when it's come to you."

"*You* are not your family, Alex. If there's one thing I've always known, it's that."

"And what about the rest?"

"Rest?"

"Marrying me." His thumbs pressed her chin up until her mouth hovered mere inches from his. "Be my partner. My friend. My wife. My life. I'll spend the rest of it—a *long* rest of it—showing you there's nothing to fear. Not if we're together. Marry me, Nikki Day."

She gave a little sigh. Looked into his eyes and finally, *finally* let go. Led from her heart.

In the end, it was the easiest thing to do. "How many times do I have to say yes?" she asked softly.

The muscle in his jaw stopped flexing. The corner of his lips quirked upward, and the chocolate of his eyes went soft and dark. "Until we walk up the aisle after the minister pronounces us husband and wife."

"Yes," she whispered, her eyes drifting closed as his lips settled on hers. Joy swelled inside her, threatening to burst out of her skin. "Yes. Yes. Yes…"

Epilogue

"I knew this place would look amazing in the summer, but I didn't expect this." Nikki sat forward in her seat as Alex drove up the graded road outside of Lucius to the Tucker cabin.

Built of enormous logs on an aging stone foundation, the cabin looked the same. But the green meadow, dotted with endless wildflowers in every color of the spectrum, surrounded by sky-high evergreens, took what had once looked forbidding and made it impossibly welcoming.

"No wonder it gets used for honeymoons," she murmured. "It's something out of a fairy tale."

Alex sent her an indulgent smile. "I'm not sure what it says about us that we were both set on coming back here. We could have gone anywhere in the world for a honeymoon, but we came to Lucius."

Nikki grabbed his hand, threading her fingers through his. Lucius would always be a special place for her, and now the only memories it would hold would be the ones she intended to create with Alex. They'd waited three months since their wedding for this trip. "I could go anywhere in this world, or nowhere at all. As long as I'm with you, it doesn't matter."

He parked near the door and climbed out of the car and stretched. It had been a long drive from Cheyenne. They could easily have flown, but they were in no rush. He'd arranged to be away from Huffington for two weeks.

And he hadn't even brought his cell phone.

She watched him through the windows as he rounded the car to her side and wondered how long she'd be able to hide the fact that she'd hidden *her* cell phone in a pocket inside her suitcase.

Probably not long.

Keeping even surprises secret from Alex was too difficult to maintain for long.

He didn't open her door first. Instead, he opened the back door. She looked over her shoulder, and everything inside her went soft, as it always did whenever she watched Alex with April. She looked forward to seeing that devotion on his face with all of their children, if they were blessed with more.

Their daughter had slept nearly the entire drive, and it would be a miracle if she slept at all that night. Nikki didn't care. There'd been no question of them leaving April behind. She was only two months old, after all. She needed her mom and dad.

Her mom and dad needed her.

Alex capably released the carrier from the car seat base that stayed secured in the vehicle. He lifted out his daughter, carrier and all, and she didn't even whimper. Just kept sleeping like the angel she often…wasn't.

Nikki started to open her door, but Alex beat her to it. He still had a tendency to treat her as if she were made of glass.

Until they were in bed, that is.

She wasn't complaining.

But now, he handed her the carrier. "Hold her."

She thought he intended to get their luggage, but he didn't. As soon as she'd grasped the carrier's sturdy handle, he swept her up into his arms.

Nikki laughed, grabbing the carrier closer to her. "Hey, we don't need to be airlifted around anymore. Remember?"

"Humor me."

If it put that crinkling smile in his eyes, she'd agree to anything. He carried her and April up the steps, and she reached down to find the door key that—just as last time—was hidden inside the old mailbox on the wall next to the door. When she'd fitted it into the lock, the door swung open and Alex carried her inside.

It was exactly the same.

The enormous red couch. The lovers' tub. The dominating fireplace and the velvet-covered bed, visible on the other side. The lurid mirrors.

Alex carried her to the couch and set her on it. "How long do you think we have?"

Nikki peered at their daughter, the love inside her so overwhelming she couldn't imagine ever taking it for granted. She carefully adjusted the lightweight blanket and watched April's tiny bow mouth purse, working even in her sleep.

It wouldn't be long before their daughter would wake, ravenous. She'd arrived in the world right on time in a speedy delivery as if she'd never caused a bit of fuss during the pregnancy. "An hour," Nikki whispered. "Maybe."

"That'll do." His smile was devilish. He drew Nikki to her feet. Caught her mouth with his and pulled her around the fireplace.

But he didn't tear off her clothes, didn't get rid of his own as expediently as he usually did. He just stood there, his hands cupping her shoulders.

"Alex?"

"I'm glad we came here. Not because of the satin sheets, or the mirrors."

Her heart squeezed all over again. "Because it started here?"

"It started the first day you agreed to work for me, three years ago last April. But here is where it finally came together." His thumb drifted down her cheek in a familiar caress that would tug at her heart in fifty years as surely as it did now. "This is where I realized how important you were to me. Why my life wasn't right without you."

She laid her palm against his jaw. How she loved him! She was so grateful for the chance they'd been given. "It doesn't matter where it started," she said softly. "At Huffington, or here. What matters is that we both finally believe that it is not going to end."

He lowered his head, his forehead resting against hers. "You've never asked why I didn't give you a wedding present."

They'd married a month before April was due, in the lovely little community church in Weaver. Her family had packed the aisles, leaving barely enough room for the one guest who'd come from Alex's side.

Valerie. Sans Hunter, and yet again trying to make a fresh start without him in her life. Nikki wished the other woman success.

Eyes closed now, savoring the moment with her husband, Nikki smiled a little. Her hands drifted down the front of his shirt, toying with the buttons. "I thought the RHS shares you bought from Hunter were my wedding present."

His hands threaded through her hair. "Those, too. It was your idea, after all. Beating them at their own game. Instead of convincing Hunt to vote the way I wanted him to, I convinced him to sell his shares in RHS to me, and voted down my father's acquisition plans for both Macfield and Huffington myself. Hunt never cared where his money came from, as long as it came. Selling to me meant he didn't have to deal with my father any longer."

"I still can't believe you bought into Reed Health Systems."

"If sitting across a board table from my father saves the future of the Huffington family, then it's worth it. I'd rather be in *his* business than have him in mine. He's resigned his chairmanship effective at the end of the year, anyway. He recovered from the heart attack, but it left its mark. My uncle who's been running the Philadelphia shop will take over when he goes."

"Someday *you* could be chairman of the board of RHS," she pointed out.

He shook his head. "I'm a Reed and RHS may be my heritage, but it's not my present and it sure in hell isn't my future. *That* is with you and our baby. The gift you've given me. A family. A real one. But that doesn't answer the matter of my wedding gift to you."

She sighed, tilting her head back, luxuriating in his touch. "I don't need gifts, Alex. I have everything I want."

"Well, you're getting this one." His hand moved, and he slid the old-fashioned cabin key down the V-neck of her ivory T-shirt, tucking it between her breasts.

She shook her head a little. "What are you talking about?" From the other room, they heard April's soft snuffle.

"I bought the cabin. For you." He slowly drew his fingers out of her shirt. "For us. So we can always have this place to escape to. We'll remodel and redecorate however you want. Put up walls for a proper bedroom, if nothing else. But I do have one request."

She twined her arms around his broad shoulders, fitting herself against him. "Anything."

"The satin sheets?"

She pressed her mouth to his, a vision dancing in her mind—of them years from now dragging April to Lucius for summer vacations and winter sleigh rides. "What about them?"

Still holding her, he leaned over and threw back the red velvet bedspread with one arm, before settling her in the center of the wide bed and that slippery, smooth silver satin. "They stay."

She clasped her arms around him and smiled, absorbing the love that shone from his melted-chocolate eyes.

Alex would always be driven to succeed. And she'd always send up a quick prayer of thanks when, at the end of the day, he walked in the door of the house they'd bought just outside of Cheyenne, alive and well.

But first and foremost, he'd be hers.

And she'd be his.

"Absolutely," she agreed, laughing with a delight that overflowed her very soul.

A lifetime wouldn't be long enough for the discoveries they were constantly making about each other. "The satin sheets stay. That naughty mirror will have to go. At least the etchings on the border, or someday we'll be spending time explaining it to April—"

"Oh, God." He sounded horrified at the idea, and Nikki laughed all over again.

"But the tub," she whispered. "I've got plenty of ideas when it comes to the tub…."

* * * * *

Coming in October to

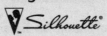

SPECIAL EDITION™

the fourth book in the new continuity

MOST LIKELY TO...

Eleven Students. One reunion. And a secret
that will change everyone's lives.

THE PREGNANCY PROJECT

(SE #1711)

by reader favorite

Victoria Pade

He was her last chance to have a baby—but his
bedside manner left a lot to be desired. Could
the patient's gentle nature prove to be the best
medicine for the physician's scarred heart?

*Don't miss this compelling story—only from
Silhouette Books.*

Available at your favorite retail outlet.

Where love comes alive™

COMING NEXT MONTH